SONS OF

The
PROPHET

a novella

ENCOURAGEMENT

FRANCINE RIVERS

TYNDALE HOUSE PUBLISHERS, INC.
CAROL STREAM, ILLINOIS

To men of faith who serve

in the shadow of others.

✦   ✦   ✦

Visit Tyndale's exciting Web site at www.tyndale.com

Check out the latest about Francine Rivers at www.francinerivers.com

TYNDALE and Tyndale's quill logo are registered trademarks of Tyndale House Publishers, Inc.

The Prophet

Designed by Luke Daab

Cover design by Luke Daab

Edited by Kathryn S. Olson

Library of Congress Cataloging-in-Publication Data

Rivers, Francine, 1947–
    The prophet / Francine Rivers.
        p. cm. — (Sons of encouragement ; 4)
    ISBN-13: 978-0-8423-8268-7 (hc)
    ISBN-10: 0-8423-8268-2 (hc)
    1. Amos (Biblical prophet)—Fiction.   2. Bible. O.T.—History of Biblical events—
Fiction.   3. Religious fiction.   I. Title
    PS3568.I83165P76 2006
    813'.54—dc22   2006007811

Printed in the United States of America

11   10   09   08   07   06
 9   8   7   6   5   4   3   2   1

a c k n o w l e d g m e n t s

FROM the beginning of my writing career, my husband, Rick, has blessed me continually with his encouragement. Without him, I might not have had the courage to send in the first manuscript that began my journey as a writer. He listens to my ideas, makes space for me in his office at Rivers Aviation, brews great coffee, and edits the final draft. He even builds me a fire on cold mornings. I delight in his company!

The Lord has also blessed me with encouraging friends. I want to mention two in particular: Peggy Lynch and Pastor Rick Hahn. I can't even count the number of times I've called Peggy or Pastor Rick to ask where a particular Scripture passage is and/or to check my understanding of God's Word. Both of these friends have loved Jesus since childhood, have a passion for God's Word, and are gifted teachers. Each has played an important part in bringing my husband and me to Jesus, and each continues to teach and encourage us in our walk with the Lord today. May the Lord bless you both for your kindness!

I offer special thanks to Peter Parsons for his great love of Amos. He was the first to encourage me to write this prophet's story. May this rendering of the prophet's story be all you hoped it would be, Peter.

I want to thank my editor, Kathy Olson, and Ron Beers for their continued support and encouragement. I greatly appreciate their willingness to work with me to strengthen each story. There are so many people at Tyndale who have encouraged and prayed for me over the years. From the beginning of our relationship, I have felt part of the team.

And I want to thank all those who have prayed for me over the years and through the course of this particular project. When I'm assailed by doubts, which often happens, I remember you are praying. May the Lord bless each of you for your tender hearts.

May Jesus Christ be glorified in this story that came from His Word. Let this story fire your interest in studying the biblical book of Amos. And may each reader be encouraged to love the Lord with heart, mind, soul, and strength. Jesus is life abundant and everlasting. Take up your cross and follow Him with rejoicing.

DEAR READER,

This is the fourth of five novellas on biblical men of faith who served in the shadows of others. These were Eastern men who lived in ancient times, and yet their stories apply to our lives and the difficult issues we face in our world today. They were on the edge. They had courage. They took risks. They did the unexpected. They lived daring lives, and sometimes they made mistakes—big mistakes. These men were not perfect, and yet God in His infinite mercy used them in His perfect plan to reveal Himself to the world.

We live in desperate, troubled times when millions seek answers. These men point the way. The lessons we can learn from them are as applicable today as when they lived thousands of years ago.

These are historical men who actually lived. Their stories, as I have told them, are based on biblical accounts. For the facts we know about the life of Amos, see the biblical book that bears his name.

This book is also a work of historical fiction. The outline of the story is provided by the Bible, and I have started with the information provided for us there. Building on that foundation, I have created action, dialogue, internal motivations, and in some cases, additional characters that I feel are consistent with the biblical record. I have attempted to remain true to the scriptural message in all points, adding only what is necessary to aid in our understanding of that message.

At the end of each novella, we have included a brief

study section. The ultimate authority on people of the Bible is the Bible itself. I encourage you to read it for greater understanding. And I pray that as you read the Bible, you will become aware of the continuity, the consistency, and the confirmation of God's plan for the ages— a plan that includes you.

Francine Rivers

THEY were coming.

They moved swiftly, keeping low to the ground, silent streaks of black in the fading light. Amos didn't have to see them or hear them to know the enemy was closing in. He felt it, through instinct honed by years of living in the wilderness. Three sheep were missing—the same stubborn dam who so frequently troubled him, and her twin lambs. He must act quickly.

Calling to his flock, he watched them race toward him. They sensed his urgency and followed him into the fold. He closed the gate behind them and secured it. Assured of their safety, he was free now to go after the lost ones.

He ran, and the stones in his pouch rattled. He took one out and fitted it to his sling.

A lamb bleated, and he raced toward the frightened sound. The foolish dam remained intent upon having her own way. Rather than stay in the green pastures to which he led her, she continued to choose brambles and brush.

Amos saw the wolves. He raised his arm, the sling emitting a high-pitched whir before he released the stone. With a yelp of pain, the pack leader went down heavily, but quickly regained his feet.

Amos came on. Snarling, the wolf advanced in a low crouch, hackles raised. The others circled, teeth bared, determined. The dam did not move, frozen in fear, while her helpless lambs bleated in confusion and fear. When one ran, a wolf leapt at it. Before it could sink its jaws into the young throat, Amos sent another stone flying. It struck hard and true. The wolf dropped, a stone embedded in its skull.

Most of the others fled, but the alpha remained to challenge. Amos hurled his club, and struck it hard in the hip. With another cry of pain, the wolf limped into the brush and disappeared.

The lamb lay still. Amos lifted it tenderly, examining it. No wounds, but it was limp in his arms. Shock and fear had killed it.

He sighed heavily. How many times had this dam led others into danger? How many times had he rescued her, only to have to hunt her down again? He cared deeply for all his sheep, even this dam who habitually caused trouble. But he could not allow her to go on leading others into the jaws of predators.

The other twin bleated pitifully. The dam paid little attention. Safe now, she moved stiff-necked, ruminating as she gazed once at Amos before heading toward the brush. Shaking his head, Amos placed the dead lamb on the ground, unsheathed his knife, and went after her.

When the deed was done, Amos felt only sorrow. If only she had stayed close to him, he would not have found it necessary to end her life for the sake of the others.

He carried the surviving twin back to the fold.

✦   ✦   ✦

Another dam accepted the lamb. Having finished nursing, the lamb cavorted with others. He was old enough to nibble tender shoots of grass. Amos leaned on his staff and watched the lambs play. He laughed at their antics. All seemed well.

A bleat of distress drew his attention. One of the rams

had cast himself in a low spot. He lay in a hollow, feet in the air.

"Easy there, old man." Twice, the ram kicked Amos. Taking strong hold, Amos heaved him over and lifted him.

The ram couldn't walk.

"Hold on." Amos held him firm between his knees. He massaged the animal until the circulation returned to its legs. "Go ahead." He gave the ram a push.

The ram stumbled once and then walked stiff-legged, head up, ignoring Amos.

"Next time, find a flat place to rest."

Amos turned from the ram and made a quick count of the flock. His mouth tightened.

The lamb was missing again.

Amos called to his sheep and led them to the shade of the sycamore trees. They would settle quickly there in the heat of the afternoon. He scanned the area, hoping the lamb would come scampering back.

A buzzard made a wide circle overhead. It wouldn't be long until another joined it. There was no time to waste. Leaving the ninety-nine others, Amos headed west. Staff in hand, he wove his way among the rocks and brambles, searching, hoping he would find the lamb before a predator did. The wolf pack had kept its distance, but there were lions in these hills.

Coming to a rise, Amos spotted the lamb standing near some bushes. As he approached, he saw its wool had snagged in a thornbush. One hard tug, and the lamb could have freed itself, but it was not in his nature to do so. Instead, the animal would stand still until rescue came— or a predator, eager to make a meal of him.

Amos stood grimly, considering what to do. Less than

a week ago, he had been forced to kill the lamb's mother. He had known for months he might have to dispatch her, but held off doing so because she was perfectly proportioned with well-set, alert eyes and was one of the strongest sheep in his flock. But her stubborn habits had endangered the entire flock. Half a dozen times he had rescued her and her offspring. He had hoped to give the lambs more time to be fully weaned and on their own. Now, it seemed he had waited too long, for the lamb had learned his mother's bad habits.

"It's this or death, little one." Amos took a stone from his pouch, weighing it in his hand. Too heavy and it would kill the lamb; too light and it would not serve to discipline him. Amos swung his sling and released the stone, striking the lamb in a front leg, just above the knee. With a startled bleat of pain, the lamb went down.

Tears burning, Amos went to the wounded lamb and knelt. "I am here, little one. I would rather wound you myself than see you come to greater harm." He knew after a gentle examination that the leg was broken, but not shattered. It would heal. "You belong with the flock, not out here on your own where death will find you." He worked quickly, binding the leg and tugging the lamb free of the brambles. "I know I hurt you, but better you suffer an injury that will heal than become dinner for a prowling lion." He ran his hand gently over the lamb's head. "You will learn to stay close to me where you're safe." He cupped the lamb's head and breathed into its face. "No struggling or you will cause yourself more pain." He gently lifted the lamb onto his shoulders and carried him back to the flock.

The goats grazed in the hot sun, but the sheep still

rested in the shade, ruminating. Amos sat on a flat rock that gave him a full view of the pasture. Lifting the lamb from his shoulders, he held it close. "You will learn to trust me and not think you can find better forage on your own. I will lead you to green pastures and still waters." He took a few grains of wheat from the scrip he wore at his waist and shared his food with the lamb. "Sometimes I must wound in order to protect." He smiled as the lamb ate from his hand. "You will get used to my voice and come when I call." He rubbed the notch in the lamb's ear. "You bear my mark, little one. You are mine. Let me take care of you."

Amos looked out over the others. They were content. There was still plenty of grass. One more night here, he decided. Tomorrow he would move the flock to new pastures. Too long in one pasture, and the sheep grew restless and would not lie down. They would begin to compete for space. Too many days in one field and the flies and gnats would begin to pester. Conditions must be just right for his sheep to be at peace.

Later in the afternoon, the sheep rose from their rest and grazed again. Two dams pushed at each other. Amos carried the lamb with him as he separated them with his staff. "There's forage enough for both of you." He stood between them until they settled. His presence soothed them, and they lowered their heads to graze.

From Jerusalem to the high country, Amos knew every pasture as well as he knew his family's inheritance in Tekoa. He worked part of each year in the sycamore groves near Jericho in order to pay for grazing rights. Incising sycamore figs to force ripening was tedious work, but he wanted only the best pasturage for his flock. Dur-

ing the winter months when the sheep were sheltered in
Tekoa, he went out to clear reeds, deepen or enlarge water
holes, and repair old or build new sheepfolds.

A dam jumped, startled by a rabbit that leapt from a
patch of grass and bounded off. She started to run, but
Amos caught her with the crook of his staff before she
could spread panic.

He spoke softly and put his hand on her to soothe her.
"I am with you. No need to fear." He carried the lamb
with him wherever he went and placed it on the ground
where it could sleep on its side in the shade. He fed it
wheat and barley and the best grass.

The old ram was cast again. He left the lamb near the
quietest dam and went to attend to the old codger. The
animal had found another hollow in which to rest. As the
ram slept, his body had rolled onto its side. Bleating
angrily, the ram kicked as Amos approached, and succeeded only in rolling onto his back, legs in the air.

Amos shook his head and laughed. "A pity you don't
learn, old man."

Belly exposed, the ram was helpless. Amos bent to the
task of righting the animal and setting it back on its feet.
He held it firmly between his knees until he was certain
the ram had feeling in his legs.

"You always find the low spots, don't you?" He massaged the legs and gave the ram a push. "Back you go.
Find a flat spot in the shade this time."

The ram walked away with wounded dignity, stiff-
legged, head in the air. He soon found a good patch of
grass.

Retrieving the lamb, Amos carried it around on his
shoulders. He felt great peace out here in the open, away

from Jerusalem, away from the marketplace and corrupt priests. But he missed his family. Sometimes he could almost hear his father's voice: *"We tend the Temple flocks, my son. It is a great honor to work for the priests."*

As a youngster, how Amos had reveled in that! Until he learned the truth about his family's relationship with the priest Heled. He sighed. Nearly twenty years had passed, but his disillusionment was as fresh as ever.

When Amos was a child, it had been a common occurrence for Joram, a servant of Heled, to come to Amos's family's home and take several blemished lambs, leaving perfect ones to replace them. When Amos asked his father where the blemished lambs were taken, he said, "To Jerusalem."

"But why does he bring us the same number of lambs he takes away?" Amos had wondered. He could make no sense of it, and his father's answers never satisfied him.

Then, during a visit to Jerusalem for a festival one year, the year he was eleven, he had watched everything that went on around the stalls his older brothers managed, and what he saw greatly disturbed him.

"Father, aren't these the lambs Joram took a week ago?"

"Yes."

"But doesn't God require lambs without blemish for sacrifice? That one has a damaged hoof, and the other over there has a spot inside its ear. I can show you."

"Be quiet, Amos!"

Confused, Amos held his tongue. He watched a priest examine a lamb. Amos went closer and saw for himself the animal was perfect, but the priest shook his head and pointed to the stalls. Frowning, the man carried the lamb he had brought for sacrifice to Amos's brother. Bani put it

in a pen and then caught the lamb with the blemish inside
its ear and handed it over. The man argued, but Bani
waved him off. When the man returned to the priest, the
new lamb was accepted, but not before the man paid a fine
for the exchange.

"Did you see that, Father? The priest—"

"Stop staring! Do you want to cause trouble?"

"But the lamb that man originally brought is better than
the one Bani gave him. God will not be pleased."

"Heled rejected the man's sacrifice. That's all you need
to know."

"But why? What was wrong with it?"

His father gripped Amos's shoulders and stared into his
face. "Never question what the priests decide! Never! Do
you understand?"

Amos winced at the pain. He did not understand, but
he knew better than to ask more questions now. His father
let go of him. As he straightened, Amos saw Heled scowl-
ing at him. He motioned to Amos's father.

"I must speak with Heled. Wait here."

Amos watched them. Heled did all the talking, and his
father kept his eyes downcast and nodded and nodded.

Ahiam grabbed Amos and spun him around. "Father
told you not to stare, didn't he? Go get feed for the
lambs."

Amos ran to do his brother's bidding.

When he came back, his father took him aside.
"Remember, priests are servants of the Lord, Amos. They
see imperfection where we do not and their decisions are
law. If you question their judgment, they will say you
question God Himself. They would bar you from the syna-
gogue and Temple. And then what would happen? No one

would have anything to do with you. You would become an outcast with no way to make a living. You would have to sell yourself into slavery."

Amos hung his head and blinked back tears.

His father squeezed his shoulder. "I know you don't understand what's happening here." He sighed. "Sometimes I wish I didn't. But you must trust me, Amos. Say nothing about the lambs, good or bad. And don't watch what Heled does. It bothers him. The priests are very powerful and must be treated with great respect. We are only hirelings paid to tend the Temple flocks. That's all. Perhaps someday we will have sheep of our own and be free again. . . ."

After that day, Amos had begun to observe everything that went on around the folds of Tekoa, in Jerusalem, and around the Temple.

Discolorations on a lamb would disappear under the care of his brothers.

"We're miracle workers!" Ahiam laughed, but when Amos surreptitiously examined one, he found the wool stiff with white stuff that rubbed off on his fingers.

"Father will have your hide," Amos told Bani.

Ahiam overheard and knocked him on his backside. "Father knows, you little runt."

The next time Joram came, Amos realized the priest's servant deliberately chose weaker lambs. As soon as Amos found his father alone, he reported what he had observed.

His father gazed out over the fields. "One lamb is much like any other."

"But that's not true, Father. You've told me yourself how every lamb is different, and—"

"We'll talk about it later, Amos. We have too much work to do right now."

But *later* never came, and every time Amos went with his father to Jerusalem, he was afraid God would do something horrible when one of those blemished lambs was offered as a sacrifice.

"What's wrong with your brother?" Heled scowled as he spoke to Ahiam.

"Nothing. Nothing is wrong with him. He's just quiet, that's all."

"Quiet . . . and all eyes and ears."

Ahiam slapped Amos hard on the back. When he gripped Amos, his fingers dug in deep and shook him as he grinned down, eyes black. "He's not used to city life yet."

"Get him used to it!" Heled walked away and then called back over his shoulder. "Or keep him away from Jerusalem altogether."

Ahiam glowered at him. "Make yourself useful. Add feed to the bins if you have to hang around here. Do something other than *watch*."

Amos worked in silence, head down, afraid. He kept to himself and kept busy for the rest of the day. He said so little, his family grew concerned when they gathered for the Passover meal.

"What's wrong, little brother? Aren't you feeling well?"

"He's upset about the lambs," Ahiam said grimly. "You'd better tell him, Father."

"Not yet."

"Why not? He's old enough to understand." Ahiam's

expression was grim. "I think he's figured out most of it on his own."

"Later."

Amos wasn't hungry. He felt like an outcast, and fought tears. But he had to know, and so he asked again. "Why does Joram take the weak lambs and leave the good ones?"

His father bowed his head.

Chin jutting, Ahiam answered. "Why slaughter a perfect lamb when one bearing a spot will do just as well?"

Ahiam's wife, Levona, hung her head as she turned the spitted lamb over the fire. "What a waste to kill a prized ram that could reproduce itself ten times over!"

For a moment, the only sound in the room was the pop and hiss of fat as it dripped into the burning coals.

No one would meet Amos's eyes. "Is our lamb perfect?"

"Of course, it's perfect!" Bani burst out. "Do you think we'd offer anything less?"

"But what about those others? the weak ones from our flock?" Amos turned to his father, then to Bani and Ahiam. "The Law says only perfect lambs are acceptable as Temple sacrifices. But Joram brought the weak ones from Tekoa, and they are the ones you exchanged today." Amos's heart beat heavily as the tension built.

Levona kept her eyes on the roasting lamb. Mishala, Bani's wife, placed the bitter herbs on the table. Bani looked at their father, expression pained.

Ahiam banged his fists on the table, making everyone jump. "Tell him, Father, or I will!"

"Who decides if the Law has been fulfilled, Amos?"

"God."

"And who speaks for God?"

"The priests."

"Yes!" Ahiam glared. "The priests! The priests decide which lamb is fit and which isn't."

His father sighed. "You saw who sent those people to our pens, Amos."

"The priests. But is this the way it's supposed to be?"

"It is the way it is." His father sounded worn down, defeated.

Fear filled Amos. "What will the Lord do? Is He satisfied?"

Ahiam poured wine. "What sign do we see that the Lord is not pleased with what is given to Him? The priests get richer each year. We are close to paying off all our family debts. The nation prospers. The Lord must be satisfied."

Bani grimaced as he ate the bitter herbs. "You have been taught as we all have, Amos—riches are the reward of righteousness."

God said He would bless those who obeyed His commands, making sure those who loved Him would have lives of abundance. Amos's father had taught him that meant a fine home, flocks and herds, orchards of fruit trees, olive trees, a vineyard, and lots of children. The priests had all of these things and more, and his father and brothers were working hard toward the same end. Should he question things he didn't understand?

Confused, disheartened, he fought against the thoughts that raced through his mind.

When his father stood, Amos did also. Tunics girded, sandals on their feet, they ate the Passover meal standing in memory of God's deliverance of the Hebrews from Egypt.

Where is God now? Amos wondered.

"Eat, Amos."

"I'm not hungry."

His father dipped unleavened bread into the salt water that represented the tears the Hebrews shed while slaves in Egypt. Everyone ate in silence. When the meal was over, Amos's father, Ahiam, and Bani sat while Levona and Mishala cleared the table and the children went into another room to play.

Ahiam glared at nothing, a muscle twitching in his cheek. Bani sat with head down.

Amos's father cleared his throat and turned to Amos. "It is time you understand what we do. You must know the whole story to understand."

Amos's heart began to beat loudly.

"Your great-grandfather fell into debt. It was a time of war, and the priests levied higher fines on guilt and sin offerings to raise money for the army. Grandfather paid what he could, but each year, the interest increased and debt grew rather than diminished. When he died, my father continued to pay on the debt. By then, we owed so much that there was no hope of ever paying it off. When my father died, the debt fell to me. Heled came to me in Tekoa and offered me a way to pay off our family disgrace. Because I did not want it to fall upon your brothers or you or any of your children, I agreed."

Ahiam's eyes darkened. "If Father had not agreed, we would all be slaves. Do you understand now, little brother?"

"There is no reason to take your anger out on him, Ahiam." His father put a hand on Amos's shoulder. "Heled hired us to tend the flocks of lambs that were brought as gifts for God."

Amos's stomach churned. "So the priests take the perfect lambs intended for God and give them to us to tend, and they give the weaker ones to people to sacrifice at the Temple."

His father's hand fell away. No one spoke.

"Yes," Ahiam said finally. "Yes, that's exactly what we do. Because we have no choice."

It was all becoming clear to Amos. He shuddered as he thought aloud. "So the priests keep the perfect lambs. They will produce valuable wool year after year. Then they force the people to buy imperfect lambs to sacrifice, so they make money that way too." He looked up at his father. "And on top of all that, they make the people pay a fine for the exchange!" Why weren't his father and brothers as outraged as he was?

Bani leaned his arms on the table and clasped his hands. "We have our inheritance back, Amos, the land that God gave our fathers who came across the Jordan River."

"The debt is almost clear," his father added quietly. "By the time you are sixteen, it will be paid off."

Ahiam stood and turned his back.

Bani glanced up at Ahiam and then spoke softly. "They are priests, Amos. We dare not question them. Do you understand?"

"We serve the Lord!" Ahiam said loudly. "We tend the Temple flocks. There is honor in that."

Honor? Amos hung his head. *We're stealing from God.* Tears burned his eyes.

Their father rose and left the room.

Bani sighed. "Father had no choice. None of us have a choice."

"We're not the only ones," Ahiam said. He met Amos's

eyes, face hard. "It's been done for as long as I can remember."

"Do all the priests do the same thing?"

"Not all," Bani said.

Ahiam snorted. "But you don't hear them saying anything against those who do. God gave the tribe of Judah the scepter, but he gave the Levites the priesthood. And that's where the real power is. They can interpret the Law any way they want. They even add to it on a daily basis. They use it to squeeze the people for as much as they want. Better we stand with them than against them."

"When you're a little older, you'll be free of all this, Amos." Their father had come back into the room. "By the time you're a man, we will be done with it."

"We live better now than we did before our agreement with Heled," Ahiam said, but his eyes were dark with bitterness.

Anger grew inside Amos. "It's not right what the priests did to you, Father. It's not right!"

"No, it isn't. But we adjust to the way things are, my son. And they have been this way for a long, long time."

Shaken, Amos was left to wonder whether God was truly holy. Was He truly just? If so, why did He allow these things to go on in His own Temple? Why would a righteous, holy God reward corrupt, scheming men who misused His Name?

The revelations of that night had sowed seeds of anger that sent shoots of bitterness into Amos's heart. From that day on, Amos hated the required visits to Jerusalem. He paid no more attention to the priests and what they said, focusing instead on visiting his brothers, their wives and children. He gave the offerings required by Law only because they were necessary for business. Amos always chose the best lamb and sought out a priest who examined the animal properly. He did it to save the fine, rather than to please God.

In his mind, it was a small rebellion, a way of getting back at Heled without risking retaliation against his father.

These days, he didn't think about God anymore. With all he had seen around the Temple pens, he believed God had forgotten about them, and all the rituals were to profit men rather than to honor a silent monarch who reigned so far up in the heavens. Did God see? Did God hear? Did He care what went on in His own Temple?

✦   ✦   ✦

Amos's father had not lived long enough to see the family debt paid off. Long after he was buried, Bani and Ahiam continued to work for the priests at the stalls in Jerusalem. Years of habit, convenience, and prosperity choked honesty. Amos remained among the shepherds of Tekoa, tending his flock of goats and sheep.

He felt at peace in the hills and dales of Judah, alone with his sheep. Each year, he had grown less able to tolerate the busy streets of Jerusalem—the chattering crowds, shouting street vendors, and arguing scribes. Relieved when his obligations were completed, he would eagerly depart the confines of those great walls, returning to the open fields where the sun blazed and the wind blew, where he could breathe fresh air again.

Life was not easy, but it was simple without the intrigues, coercion, or pressures he knew his brothers lived with on a daily basis. They had spent so many years

in the stalls, tending corralled animals and dealing with
Heled and others like him, that they knew no other way to
live. They had become merchants, accustomed to trade,
and did not see the result of their labors in the same way
Amos did. They did not stand in the Temple, full of questions, angry and anguished.

Amos hated seeing humble men with barely enough to
live on cheated by priests who grew richer each year. Men
came to pray and instead found themselves preyed upon.
Maybe God didn't know what went on in His Temple.
Maybe He didn't care.

"You hardly speak, little brother. You have lived too
long with your sheep. You've forgotten how to be among
men."

"I have nothing to say." *Nothing anyone would want to
hear.*

Amos had earned enough from his flock to plant a few
olive trees and a vineyard. In time he had hired servants.
They received a share of the crops as payment for oversee-
ing the vineyard, the olive trees, and the small fields of
wheat and barley.

Amos did not have a wife, nor any desire to find one.
He was too busy working near Jericho for grazing rights,
tending his growing flock, and pruning and incising the
fruit of his sycamore trees. He kept what he needed and
sold the rest as cattle fodder. At least, he was free now.
Free of Heled's hold, free to make his own choices. He
knew better, though, than to show disrespect—lest a fine
be created to enslave him again.

As his flock had grown, Amos asked Bani and Ahiam to
send their sons to help. "Within a few years, each will

have a small flock of his own. What they do with it will be up to them." But it was an opportunity to break free.

Bani sent Ithai, and Ahiam sent Elkanan, and Amos taught them all he knew about tending a flock. When he felt they were ready to be sent out alone, he gave them each a ram and ten ewes with which to start.

"Whatever increase comes shall be yours." Maybe they would take to the life as he did and not follow in the ways of their fathers.

He knew little of what happened in the kingdom while he tended his flock, but when he made his pilgrimages to Jerusalem, his brothers told him what they had heard during the months he had been in distant pastures.

Judah was prospering under King Uzziah's rule, though relations with the ten tribes of Israel were still hostile. The tribes that had broken away from Solomon's foolish son continued to worship the golden calves in Bethel and Dan. Jeroboam II now ruled, and Samaria had become a great city a mere two-day journey from Jerusalem. King Jeroboam had taken back lost lands and cities from Lebo-hamath to the Dead Sea, expanding Israel's boundaries to those from the time of King David and King Solomon. In a bold move to gain more power, he captured Gilead, Lodebar, and Karnaim, all important fortress cities along the King's Highway, thus controlling the major trade route from the Tigris-Euphrates river valley to the Gulf of Aqaba and Egypt. Trade now flourished with the safe passage of caravans from Gabal and Syria to the north and Egypt and Arabia to the south.

From boyhood, Amos had witnessed King Uzziah's work going on throughout Judah. The king mended Judah's defenses, reorganized and better equipped his

army, built towers in Jerusalem at the Corner Gate and the
Valley Gate, and fortified the buttresses. He had also built
towers in the wilderness to keep watch over the Philistines
and Edomites. Work crews made cisterns so that there
would be water wherever the army moved. When Uzziah
went to war against the Philistines, he triumphed and tore
down the walls of Gath, Jabneh, and Ashdod. Slaves now
bent to the task of rebuilding fortress cities that would
guard the trade route called the Way of the Sea.

Amos's home, Tekoa, was only seven miles from Jerusalem, but far enough away for him to turn his mind to
his own endeavors. Amos saw the changes in Jerusalem
and in the countryside as he moved his flock from one
pasture to another, but he spent little time contemplating
the ways of kings and nations. What use in leaning on
his own understanding when he had none? Why trouble
his mind with matters over which he had no control?
Could he change anything that happened in Judah, let
alone Assyria or Egypt or Israel, for that matter? No!
While his brothers praised Uzziah or fretted over the
threat of enemies, Amos concentrated on his sheep. He
brought tithes and offerings to the priests, visited briefly
with his brothers and their families, and then returned to
Tekoa, then out into the pasturelands with his flock. He
felt at home there.

Out in the open with his sheep, he felt free, even
though he knew that freedom could be easily stripped
from him. Out in the open Amos could believe in God. In
Jerusalem, seeing and hearing the priests living any way
they chose while claiming to represent God, Amos grew
disheartened. Why study the Law when the priests could
add to it any day they pleased? And then there were the

traditions to add an even greater burden! He preferred
a few select psalms written by David, a king who had
grown up as a shepherd. David had understood the pleasures of walking over the land, tending his sheep, sleeping
under stars scattered across the night sky.

Sometimes, when the sheep were restless or disturbed,
Amos would play his zamoora, the reed flute he'd made,
or sing psalms to comfort them.

Each time he ventured inside the walls of Jerusalem, he
tucked away his uneasy faith, lest a priestly heel crush it.
Private, protected, precious, he kept it hidden.

And it grew in ways he did not expect.

✦   ✦   ✦

"Come, sheep!" Amos called as he headed for the fold he
had made last year. The sheep came in a rush, clustering
and following close behind him. He opened the gate and
used his rod to separate the goats into another area, then
checked each sheep carefully for injury or hint of illness.

He stretched out across the entrance while the sheep
slept safely in the fold. Amos would awaken at the
slightest change. He knew the sound of every insect spe-
cies and listened for predators. When a wolf howled from
a distant hilltop, he sat up. A lamb bleated. "Be still. I am
here."

Rising, he kept his eyes on the wolves running in the
moonlight. When they ventured closer, he used his sling
to send a well-aimed stone flying at the leader. The wolf
retreated with a yelp. The pack followed, disappearing
over the hill. The sheep rose and moved around, nervous,
trembling.

Entering the fold, Amos lifted his wounded lamb to

protect it from further injury. He held it close in his arms, stroking its head and kneading its soft ears as he spoke softly to the others. "Rest now, sheep. You've nothing to fear. I will never leave you."

He stood for a long time in their midst, waiting for them to settle and sleep like the lamb in his arms. His presence calmed them. One by one, they lay down again. He set the lamb down and went back to the narrow gate, making himself a barrier against anything that might threaten his flock. Amos closed his eyes then and slept, staff and club close at hand.

Rising with the dawn, Amos opened the gate. As each lamb passed under his rod, he stopped it and examined it. Parting the wool, he checked the skin for scabbing and ran his hands over the animal to feel for any signs of trouble. He rubbed a mixture of oil, sulfur, and tar around the eyes and nose to keep the flies away. One limped, and Amos removed a rock embedded in its hoof. Straightening, he tapped the animal with his staff and watched it bound out into the field. One tried to sneak past him. He hooked the crook of his staff around its neck and turned it back. "One day you'll learn to stand and wait."

When the last sheep was examined and tended, he lifted the wounded lamb to his shoulders, closed the gate, and went out with his flock. He led them to new green pastures. Amused, Amos watched them kick up their hooves and spread out to graze. The sheep loved finding thick tufts of grass. The lambs frolicked while the dams and rams grazed.

Leaning on his staff, Amos kept watch, finding pleasure in the contentment of his flock.

✦   ✦   ✦

Spring came, bringing with it swarms of nasal gnats hatch-
ing in vast numbers near the streams and water holes.
Amos rubbed oil over the sheep's faces to repel the
insects. But even with that remedy, the sheep shook their
heads and stamped their feet, bothered by the constant
buzzing. When one bolted, others followed. Amos usually
managed to stop them before they tangled themselves in
the brush.

He led his flock to the more arid pastures near Tekoa,
knowing the best place, for he had spent a long, cold winter month clearing rocks, tearing out brush and roots so
that more grass could grow. Rich grazing away from the
torment of flies renewed the strength of the tired sheep,
and there were trees enough to provide shade from the
heat of the day.

The lamb's leg had healed. After so many weeks of
being carried and tended, the animal had bonded to Amos.
It grazed close to him and followed wherever he went.
When he sat, the lamb rested in his shadow and ruminated.

The water holes dried in the heat of summer, but the
sheep had enough water by grazing at dawn hours when
the grass was drenched with dew. The ewes produced
plenty of milk to fatten the lambs.

Amos led the flock into Tekoa for shearing. The heavy
wool had become so thick, the weight of it could make an
animal unable to get up from the soft ground they so often
sought out for rest. Cast sheep were easy prey. Though the
sheep hated being sheared, they bounded away with
renewed vigor when the work was done. Amos handed

over the thick bundles of lanolin-scented wool to workers who would remove the burrs and debris, wash the wool, and prepare it for sale.

Amos let the sheep into the fields he had planted with grains and legumes. The animals feasted for a week, and then he led them out again to cooler pastures higher in the mountains. He knew every gully, ravine, and cave between Tekoa and the mountain meadows where he kept the flock for the rest of summer. When he found lion spoor, he put himself between the flock and the brush where the beast might hide.

Girding his loins so he could move more quickly, Amos filled his pouch with stones. A lion was the most cunning of animals—patient, watchful, seizing the perfect opportunity for a kill. Staff in hand, Amos kept close watch on the brush where one might be lying in wait. Sheep had no defense. They could not run like a gazelle, nor had they teeth or claws to fight back. Attacked, they often became so frightened and confused they scattered or, worse, stood still. He had seen sheep freeze at the roar of a lion, but run in terror when startled by a rabbit.

Listening to every bird sound, watching every movement of grass, Amos stood guard over his flock. If one of his sheep strayed even a short distance, he called. If it didn't turn back, he used the crook of his staff or threw his club.

Quail burst into the air on the opposite side of the flock. A spine-tingling roar brought Amos around.

Half the sheep scattered; the rest stood, feet planted, too terrified to move as a lioness burst from the high grass and headed straight for one of the lambs.

Amos used sling and stone to stop her. The rock struck

the lioness, and she went down heavily amid bleating, scattering sheep. Dazed only, she sprang to her feet. Amos ran at her, club in hand. Crouching, she roared in fierce frustration. When she charged him, he clubbed her. She raked her claws across his right arm as she fell. He drew his knife and ran at her, but she gained her feet, scrambled back, and clawed at him. When he did not back off, she roared in defiance and disappeared into the brush.

Panting, heart pounding, Amos sheathed his knife and retrieved his club before he checked his wounds. He staunched the blood flow quickly while keeping his eye on the bushes. The lioness would return at any opportunity. "Come, sheep!"

The flock raced to him. Rams, ewes, and lambs clustered close as he led them to safety. He kept looking for signs of the lioness. If he had one of his nephews with him, he would have tracked and killed her. But alone, he would not leave his flock unprotected with a lion so close.

The sheep quickly forgot the danger and spread out to graze. Amos tended his wounds while keeping watch, walking around them to keep them close together. The lamb followed at his heels. A domineering ewe butted another away from the best grass, and stood her ground, defending her spot. When a lamb came too close, the ewe lowered her head and charged.

Amos tapped her with his staff. "There's grass enough for all."

Looking disgruntled, she ruminated for a few minutes, but lowered her head again when the lamb came close. Amos tapped her harder. Startled, she bleated, moved to one side, and lowered her head again. This time, Amos thrashed her. When the discipline was done, the ewe

walked away with stiff-legged pride to another patch of
grass. Shaking his head, Amos kept an eye on her.

Bumping and shoving tended to cause the others to
grow nervous and then irritable. When discontent
set in, appetites waned, and the entire flock suffered.
A bullying ewe could cause more trouble to a flock than
a lion.

✦   ✦   ✦

As the end of summer approached, Amos led his sheep to
the most distant pastures in the lowlands. He had paid for
grazing rights with long hard hours, days, and weeks of
incising the sycamore fruit. Now his animals benefited
from his labors, growing fat and content.

Nights became cold. Nasal flies and insects disappeared.
Leaves turned crimson and gold. Amos built fires to keep
warm at night.

The rams came into rut. Necks swelling, they strutted
like proud monarchs among a harem. To prevent them
from injuring one another, Amos rubbed their heads with
thick grease before releasing them into the pasture. They
ran, banged heads, and glanced off each other. Often they
stumbled and landed in a heap. Confused, dazed, they
would rise, looking almost embarrassed as they stood. All
those rams could think about were the ewes! And it wasn't
long before they charged again. Stubborn, they tried to
lock horns, and Amos had to get between them with his
club.

The days grew colder, nights longer. Amos led the flock
back toward Tekoa where the sheep would spend the winter in corrals. Though he moved the flock each day, he
gave them time to lie down in green pastures and rest. He

led them through the valleys, keeping them away from the shadows where predators lay in wait. He anointed each sheep's head with oil and treated every wound, most having been inflicted upon one another.

The first sight of Tekoa always filled Amos with mixed emotions. It was refreshing to come home after long months of solitude. His time of living off the land came to an end, and he looked forward to enjoying his sisters-in-law's hot meals. But in Tekoa, he would have to tend to business, meet with other herders, deal with the market in Jerusalem as well as the corrupt priests who controlled it, and face his brothers, who complained and fretted and yet never changed their ways. He would rather spend his days tending sheep and his nights beneath the star-studded canopy of the heavens than live in the confines of a house. But even a house was preferable to the chaos and cacophony of the crowded markets near the Temple.

Amos comforted himself by making plans.

As soon as the animals were wintered and tended by trustworthy servants, and the business dealings and religious obligations over, he would go back out and survey the route for next year. He would spend a month plowing and planting the pasture near Tekoa, then move on to work in the sycamore groves in Jericho. He would pull poisonous plants, remove debris from water holes, repair folds, and hunt down and kill that troublesome lioness.

Come spring, the route would be ready for his flock.

✦   ✦   ✦

"Ithai and Elkanan left eight days ago," Eliakim told Amos. "Their lambs have already been taken to Jerusalem."

Amos trusted Eliakim, his servant, over his own family members.

"Who bought them?"

"Joram. He said he would return tomorrow in the hope you would be here."

Amos despised Joram. He was as corrupt as his master, Heled. "Did he cheat us again?"

"No."

Though Eliakim said nothing more, Amos knew he had stood by as an advisor and probably saved Amos's young nephews their profits. Had they bothered to reward Eliakim? Amos would see to it that his servant never lacked for anything. "Where are Ithai and Elkanan now?"

"They returned to Jerusalem, saying they would be back after the new moon festival."

"Was Joram pleased when he left?"

"Pleased enough."

That meant trouble had been averted. This time.

Separating the best lambs as they entered the sheepfold, Amos cut out those that had the slightest blemish. He would keep them in other pens until later.

Joram arrived two days later, eager to conduct more business. "What do you have for me?"

Amos showed him.

"These are better than the ones I've brought you."

"These are the best I have." Amos named his price.

Joram's brows rose. "We exchange lambs. We don't pay for them."

"I know. But I made it clear to you things would change when our debts were paid in full."

"Your nephews are less exacting."

"You're not dealing with my nephews."

Joram scowled at him and walked to the pen that held
the blemished lambs. "What about these?" He pointed.
"I'll take that one, and the other over there."

Both had blemishes that could easily be covered. "I've
already sold them," Amos lied.

Joram turned, eyes dark. "Heled will not be pleased
about this, Amos."

Amos tried not to show how much that news pleased
him.

"You know we have had a congenial arrangement for
years."

Congenial?

Joram raised his brows. "It has benefited all of us, has it
not?"

To say it hadn't would be to declare war on the priests
who had used his father and brothers for years. Amos
knew he must tread carefully or risk having sin and guilt
offerings levied against him for any infraction that
wretched priest could find—or invent. Even with family
debts cleared, the priest thought he owned them.

Deciding not to press his luck, Amos forced a cool smile
and spoke cautiously. "The arrangement stands, Joram.
You can have the lambs I showed you." If Joram refused,
Amos would be free to offer his lambs to other priests in
Jerusalem, priests who examined animals as though the
eye of God were upon them.

"I didn't come to trade perfect lambs for other perfect
lambs."

"It does seem a waste of time."

Joram's chin jutted out. "So you think you are more
righteous than Heled?"

"Me? Only God is higher than Heled. I merely wish to

offer you what the Lord requires for sacrifice: unblemished lambs. Why should you complain?"

"And you are an expert on the Law? You? A shepherd?" He sneered.

Heart drumming, Amos stood still, hoping his anger did not show. *Do You see, God? Do You even care about Your people?*

Dark eyes narrowed at Amos's silence. "Heled has given you every advantage, Amos, and you abuse his kindness. If not for his generosity, your family would still be in debt."

Amos understood the threat, and spoke through clenched teeth. "We paid our debt in full, at a rate higher than the Law demands."

Joram's lips whitened. "You could find yourself in debt again. Easily."

Fear coursed through Amos's body. Joram stalked him like a lion, and all Amos could do was stand defenseless. One word of indignation or rebellion and Joram would pounce, setting the teeth of his threat into motion. He could pull Amos down. The priests had done it before. They could do it again.

Amos raged inwardly while showing nothing on the outside. *So this is the way it is. The way it will always be. Freedom earned can be ripped away. This is how You would have it! Power in the hands of a few who do what they want when they want. And poor men who want to do what is right suffer. The guild of priests decides what's right and wrong. These purveyors of Your Law! They can twist it and use it any way they want. They ignore what they don't like and add what will give them profits. And they keep adding and add-*

ing until the weight of their regulations crushes us! And we
are told You are a just God.

Joram smiled, smug. "I will overlook your small show
of defiance, Amos. You have served us well—and profited
from our relationship, I might remind you. Bring whatever
you have to offer us. The other lambs will be ready for
you, and the usual stipend for your labors." He slapped
Amos on the shoulder.

The wound the lion had inflicted had not yet fully
healed and Amos winced. The sharp pain made something
snap inside him. "I have nothing for you, Joram." The
lambs might not be blemished, but he would be marked
by sin for being a party to stealing from men like himself
who had worked hard and done what they thought right
only to suffer for it.

Joram grew frustrated. "We need to add to the Temple
pens! I've brought you perfect lambs."

An indictment of himself and the priest he served. Not
that Joram cared. Not that he need care. He was safe, in
favor, a Levite born to be a priest, or to serve one. He
could play the game any way he chose for the rest of his
life and never worry about where he would find his next
meal or if he would have to sell himself into slavery to pay
an unfair debt levied by a lying priest.

"Go ahead." Amos gestured grandly toward the walled
fields surrounding his few acres of land. There were other
sheep owners in Tekoa. Perhaps one of them would enjoy
the arrangement Joram would offer. Let them add their
sheep to the Temple flocks. "Talk to the owners over there
and there and there." Thousands of sheep grazed in the
pastures of Tekoa. Most belonged to the priests and the
king. "These sheep belong to me, Joram. I have built this

flock from the portion I earned. And I've already made plans for them."

"What's wrong with you, Amos? After all these years . . ."

Because he didn't know, he lied. "I guess I feel the eyes of the Lord upon me."

Joram's face went deep red. "Oh, you think you're that important. Well, someone's eye is on you. Mine!" Cursing him, Joram turned on his sandaled heel and strode away.

Amos sat and buried his head in his hands. *Will You allow them to strip me of all I've worked for, Lord? Is that Your justice and mercy?*

✦   ✦   ✦

The next morning, Amos headed for Jerusalem. He carried extra provisions for the poor, and one perfect lamb on his shoulders while driving six goats along the road ahead of him. Beggars sat before the gate, calling out for alms. Some were tricksters who had found an easy way to make a living, but others, in truth, were in dire need.

A crippled man hobbled toward him. "Good Amos. Have you anything for a poor old man?"

"A blessing upon you, Phineas. How is your wife? your daughters?" Amos gave him a pouch of grain and sycamore figs.

"Well. A blessing upon you for asking, Amos. Has it been a good year for you?"

Phineas had once been a shepherd. A boar had wrecked one leg and almost taken his life. Now, he was relegated to begging to survive. "I had to put down a dam. She kept leading others astray."

"I had a few of those in my time."

Amos had placed a few shekels in the bag as well, knowing Phineas would find them later and squeeze them for all the good they could provide. "May the Lord bless and multiply this gift, and make it last a month."

"And a greater blessing upon you, my friend. May the Lord our God smile upon you for your kindness."

Amos had seen no evidence that God smiled on anyone but the priests who stole from poor men like this one. He gave other gifts to the poor he recognized, then entered the city.

The goats brought a good price in the market. From there, he took the lamb to the Temple, where he sought out a priest who didn't know him. The lamb was deemed acceptable. *One honest priest,* Amos thought cynically. His obligations complete, he went to see his brothers.

As Amos left the Temple, he put a shekel in the plate of a blind man.

The man felt the coin eagerly and grinned. "Thank you for your kindness."

"Consider yourself blessed that you do not have to witness what goes on inside this place," Amos said as he walked away.

+   +   +

"We've been waiting for you." Bani glared, face flushed with anger. "You were supposed to bring us more lambs!"

Clearly, Joram had assumed he would think things over and capitulate. "I don't have any lambs to bring."

"What do you mean, you have no lambs?" Ahiam stared.

"I'm building my flock. The wool will—"

"Wool?" Bani came to the fence. "Why did you do that? There's more money in—"

"Have you seen the crowds?" Ahiam glared. "There's money to be made. And we need more lambs!"

"Crowds need to eat. I sold a half-dozen goats in the market."

Ahiam grabbed Amos's robe. "Joram said you insulted him. I didn't believe him. Now, I'm wondering!"

"Don't wonder." Amos tried to jerk free. "I offered him the best of the flock, and he refused."

Ahiam let go of him. "What's the matter with you, Amos? What's happened?"

"We removed the yoke, Ahiam, but you and Bani have become accustomed to it!" He stormed away.

Though his brothers called out to him, he didn't turn back. He wanted to get away from the stalls, away from the Temple, and out of the city. He gave offerings because it was expected, because his father had done it before him, and his father before that back to the time of Moses.

But what did it all mean?

He had heard the stories from the time he was a boy, but now he found himself wondering if God really existed. Maybe the priests taught their lessons merely to exert control over the people.

"God is righteous!"

"God is just!"

"God is holy!"

Amos wanted to shout, *Then why don't I see it in Your Temple? Why is there so little evidence of righteousness, justice, holiness among the priests who serve in Your name?*

"Look around you, Amos!" his brothers would say. "See how God blesses Judah. See how He blesses us."

Amos sneered as he strode through the city streets, heading for the Sheep Gate. What about the nations

around Judah? What about Israel? They bowed down to
idols and prospered even more, no longer bothering to
come to Jerusalem to worship. Jeroboam's golden calf still
stood in Bethel and another in Dan, and what had God
done about that? Nothing! The apostates grew richer and
more powerful each year.

Amos could make no sense of it.

Lying beneath a canopy of stars, it was not difficult to
believe God existed. But here, in Jerusalem—God's holy
city—the animal pens, the courts, the Temple were all
putrid with the stench of sin. The priests levied fines for
infractions written the day before. They laid down law
after law until not even a camel could carry all their
scrolls!

*If You are sovereign, why doesn't justice reign? Why are
the humble crushed by the proud, the poor impoverished by
the rich? Why are those who hold the power never held
accountable for anything? Why don't You keep Your word?*

Tears almost blinding him, Amos pressed his way
through the crowd. "Let me through! Let me out!" All he
wanted was to escape, to get away from this place that
filled him with such confusion and anguish. Only seven
miles to walk and he would be in Tekoa.

Dusk gave way to night, but the moon lighted his way.
When he reached town, he didn't go to his house, but to
the walled pasture.

Eliakim stood guard. He turned to Amos in surprise.
"I didn't expect you back for a few days."

"I finished my business there." He wished he never
had to go back, but the Law required . . .

Amos heard a familiar bleat. He put his hand on
Eliakim's shoulder. "The Lord bless you, Eliakim."

"And you, my lord."

Opening the gate, Amos entered the fold. The lamb he had wounded came to him. Hunkering down, he smiled and rubbed its face. "Rest now. I'm here."

Weary, he stretched out on the ground outside the latched gate. He put his hands behind his head and looked up at the stars. He would leave in the morning and head back out to go over his route. He needed to dig another water hole and stack more rocks for the fold on the mountain. After that, he would work in the sycamore groves to expand his grazing rights near Jericho.

The next morning, he refilled his leather scrip with grain, raisins, and almonds and set out.

And then God spoke to him, shattering all the plans Amos had made.

TWO

AMOS had never heard the Voice before, but the marrow of his bones and the blood that ran in his veins recognized it. His body shook as God whispered:

I am.

The air he inhaled tingled in his lungs, as though he had been dead and now suddenly came to life. Throwing himself on his face, Amos covered his head with his hands.

Elohim. El Elyon. El Roi.

Power and majesty. Above all gods. King of all creation.
A quickening lit Amos's soul. He was in God's presence, surrounded by Him, immersed in His Spirit, imbued by Him. Even as Amos tried to flatten himself on the earth, he was fully exposed. God knew everything about him, from first thought to final terror.

Adoni. Qedosh Yisrael. El Olam.

Head over all. Holy One of Israel. Everlasting God.
Amos cried out in fear and pleaded for his life, his voice muffled against the grass-covered earth. He had fled Jerusalem in anger and despair, doubting God even existed, let alone saw or cared what happened in His Holy City. He had even cast blame upon the Lord for the sins men committed against one another. And now this! Surely God would kill him.

Yahweh Tsidkenu. Yahweh Shammah. Attiq Yomin.

*Righteous God. Present always. Ancient of Days, Ruler
of all, Judge of the nations.*

"No more. I am a dead man."

You live.

Amos wept, the dry heart within him fluttering and
drowning in the flood of revelation.

See. Hear.

Amos felt lifted by unseen hands. He saw the Temple
on Mount Zion. There was a sound like a lion's roar, but it
wasn't like any lion Amos had ever heard as he guarded
his sheep in the wilderness. This roar was filled with
wrath. The sound grew louder, making the hair rise on the
back of his neck and his blood go cold. Even the land felt
the sound, for the ground rippled and rose and fell like a
blanket shaken clean. Though people screamed and ran,
they could not escape judgment.

Thunder crashed from Jerusalem, and came down like
a wave filling the fields, valleys, plains. The sky turned
bronze. The lush pastures of Mount Carmel withered and
died. Streams dried. Water holes evaporated, their basins
cracking, leaving nothing but dust. Sheep, cattle, goats lay
dead, carrion birds picking at their drying carcasses. Confused, trembling with fear, Amos found himself in the midst
of it; the unrelenting sun beat down on his head. Wilting to
the ground, he panted like a deer thirsting for water.

And the Word came to him, blessings and curses written down generations ago, long forgotten. His mind drank
in living water.

Opening his eyes, Amos found himself on his knees.

Raising his head, he looked around. Everything was as it had been; the rich pasture, the water hole, his pack just where he had dropped it. Bowing his head to the ground, he sobbed in relief.

Had it been a dream? A thought turned sour in his mind? The Voice! He had not imagined the Voice. Or had he?

Weak-kneed, Amos rose and went to the stream. Hunkering down, he cupped his hands and splashed water over his face. Maybe he had a fever.

I have given you a vision of what is to come.

"But why? Why me? What good would showing a poor shepherd do? Is it in my power to change anything? No!"

Amos rubbed his eyes, wishing he could rub away the images that still flickered in his mind. He heard the echo of the lion's roar and the screams in his head. Sinking back on his heels, he waited until his heart slowed its wild beat and his breathing calmed. On shaking legs, he went back to the water hole. Work would make him feel better. Work would fill his mind. He spent the last hours of daylight cutting and pulling reeds that might spread and choke the water hole. His sheep must have good water to drink. Cool, still waters were best, for the ripples of a stream frightened them.

The more determined he was not to think about the vision, the more his mind turned back to it. Again and again, over and over, it held his mind captive.

When the sun cast spears of color in the west, he set up his camp and sat in the doorway of his small tent. He had not eaten since early morning. Though he had little appetite, he forced himself to eat a small barley cake, a few dates, and sycamore figs.

A wolf howled.

Brush rustled close by.

Wind whispered softly. Night fell away in a blaze of
light. And Amos knew. . . . "No, Lord, please . . ." He
groaned as he felt hands lifting him again. Weariness fell
away and his entire being awakened, absorbing everything around him.

Remember Gilead.

Horror filled him. "No, Lord. Please. I know what happened there. . . ."

He stood in the midst of people running. They screamed
and scattered as the Aramean army advanced. Warriors
swung their swords, making no distinction between men,
women, and children. They came like sledges, scraping
over the wounded, crushing them beneath their feet. The
ground drank Israel's blood.

Amos covered his face. "Stop them! Lord, stop them!"
He could hear screams of terror, cries of pain, and moans
of the dying. Sobbing, Amos covered his ears. A man
raised his hand in a plea for mercy just as a soldier lopped
his arm off, then hacked him down with glee. Amos
longed to grab a sword and fight back, but he could not
move. He could only see, hear, smell. . . .

Carnage, everywhere, carnage.

Ben-hadad of Damascus, King of Aram, shouted commands. "Kill the vermin! Kill them all!"

Warriors beat down the people of Gilead like stalks of
wheat—cut, threshed, and blown to the wind.

When the attack ended, brutal laughter echoed across
the devastated land. Ben-hadad rode over the body of a

child, his fist raised in triumph, as though defying the God of heaven and earth.

Bodies bloated in the sun. Flies buzzed. Maggots squirmed. The smell of death filled Amos's nostrils. "My people. My people . . ."

Sobbing, he dropped to his knees and wretched violently. When the wave of sickness passed, he raised his head slowly, exhausted.

All was peaceful. Above him stars shone brightly against the canopy of night.

Anger swelled. "Why didn't You save them? They were Your people!" He raised his arms and cried out. "Why do You show me these things?"

The people of Damascus have sinned again and again, and I will not let them go unpunished!

Relief flooded him, and then exultation. The Lord would avenge those who had been butchered in Gilead. Amos jumped up and spread his arms wide. "Yes, Lord, yes! Let them feel the edge of the sword." He cried out as he saw a consuming fire come down from heaven, blackening the walls of a huge fortress, devouring the mighty gates of a great city. "Yes! Lay waste to them as they did in Gilead." He cheered, ecstatic. "Terrify *them*! Shatter *them* like earthenware."

Men battled in a great valley. Blades crashed, horns sounded, chariot wheels broke, spilling warriors into the fray. Horses reared and screamed, trampling their masters as the king who had threshed Gilead fell by the sword. The Aramean king lay dying, eyes staring up at heaven as he uttered a last curse against God.

Screams of pain rent the air as conquerors drove hooks through the noses of the survivors, looped ropes through the rings, tying the captives together. Amos watched the Arameans be led away like cattle, a long line of them being dragged away to Kir. "Yes, Lord! So be it. Let them reap what they have sown."

Did you enjoy this vision, My child?

"Yes, Lord, yes!" How long had he and others longed to do unto them as they had done unto the people of Gilead?

His mind and heart drank in the vision of vengeance without thought of where it might lead, or if it was pleasing to God. Nor did he think at all about the stillness that surrounded him after he made his confession. He thought about the last vision. And thought about it. Savoring it.

Let it be soon, Lord. Let it be soon.

✦   ✦   ✦

Amos awakened to rain pattering softly. He lay faceup like the dead king, staring into the darkness. The cool drops soothed his burning face. The rain stopped. Amos spread his fingers against the ground and found it dry. Groaning, he sat up and felt his face. It was dry and hot.

A fever. Nothing more.

Pushing himself up, he held his head. His stomach ached with emptiness. How long had he been unconscious? How long since he had eaten? He saw his scrip where he had dropped it. Taking it up, he pinched off a piece of barley bread. After a mouthful, he retied the scrip to his sash. Parched, he went down on his hands and knees and drank like a sheep from the stream.

He wanted to get away from this place of dreams.

Grabbing his pack, his staff, and his club, he took the route toward Jericho. He would look over the pastures between here and the sycamore groves, and make certain there were no poisonous plants or . . .

His mind wandered.

He had heard stories of Jonah, who had not been able to run from God. There were stories of how the prophet had boarded a ship to Tarshish only to be tossed overboard during a storm, then swallowed by a huge fish, and finally vomited onto the beach. "Go to Nineveh," God had told Jonah. It didn't matter how far Jonah ran or how deep in the hull of a ship he might hide, God knew where he was and what He wanted him to do. Relentless. God is relentless. Bani said Jonah still lived outside the walled city, waiting for destruction to come.

Amos shook his head. Why did he think about that now? Rumors, probably. A story his brother had heard from traveling merchants. Nothing more.

Please let it be nothing more.

Reaching the next pasture, Amos surveyed the grasses. Walking the field, he pulled up poisonous weeds and bundled them. Stacking the bundles on rocky soil, he set them on fire. As he watched the smoke rise, he heard a whisper:

İ will remove the evil from the land.

Amos pressed his hands over his ears. "It's just the wind. The wind in the grass." After a long moment, he drew his hands away tentatively and heard nothing but the crackling fire.

When the flames died down and only embers remained, Amos scooped dirt over them so that no sparks could float into the good grass that remained. He moved on the next morning.

Even as he tried to concentrate on work, the weeds, and water holes, his thoughts kept circling back to the Voice that came from without and within. Part of him waited for the Lord to speak again. Dreading it. Longing for it. He prayed he would hear it again and yet feared he would. When God spoke to a man, it was to send the poor fool on a mission or a long journey or to his death! His heart warred within him. Amos worked harder, faster. He forgot to eat until his stomach was gripped with pain.

He moved on again. When he reached the next pasture, he sat beneath a terebinth tree and did nothing. The sky grew dark before he got up and entered the sheepfold he had built two years before. A snake slithered hissing from the wall, startling him. Angry, he used his staff to break into its hiding place, loop it with the crook, and drop it to the ground where he killed it with his club. Even with its head crushed, the body writhed.

Moments later came the words:

I am the Lord your God.

Clutching his head, he wailed. "Why do You speak to me, Lord? I am a sinful man! I give You offerings to avoid trouble, not to praise Your Name. I despise Your priests. I can't wait to get out of Your Holy City. I can't stand being around Your people. I . . . I . . ."

Words of confession spilled from his lips. Doubt had consumed him since he was a boy, doubts that had grown into contempt for God's servants. Hadn't he thirsted for revenge after seeing his father weep over debts owed and

the only manner in which he could repay them? The
priests served God, didn't they? If they represented God,
then God must be to blame.

"All my life, I've been made part of schemes and thiev-
ery. When I wanted to do right, I caused trouble for my
brothers and their families." He saw a bigger truth now. It
came to him like a lamp in a dark cave, showing the secret
sins he failed to see in himself. "The trouble I caused had
nothing to do with me striving for righteousness. It came
from hate! I wanted to cut the bonds that held my family
captive to the priests, not because they were wrong but
because my pride rebelled. I have hated them. And I have
hated You because of what they do in Your Name."

Sobbing, he confessed every sin he remembered and
knew there were a thousand more he wouldn't even know.

"I am a sinful man, Lord. A sinful man deserving of
death." Eyes tightly closed, he bowed his head to the
ground.

Do not fear. I knew you before I formed you in your
mother's womb. You are Mine.

Amos waited. His muscles slowly relaxed. His stomach
stopped churning. He waited a long time before he raised
his head enough to see around him, and even longer yet
before he dared stand. He closed his eyes in gratitude.
"Holy is the Lord, and abounding in mercy."

When he lay down again, he slept the rest of the night
without dreams.

+   +   +

Amos did not hear the Voice again until he was working in
the sycamore groves. Others worked around him, talking,

laughing, but not hearing. Grasping a fig, he made a small cut. He felt the air grow warm around him. Everything went still. Sounds faded.

The people of Gaza have sinned again and again, and I will not let them go unpunished!

Amos saw the Philistines leading whole villages of Israelites away from their burning homes. Using whips, they forced the people to march to Edom, where they sold them as slaves.

Indignation choked him. "Our brothers make profit on our misery!" Edomites were descendants of Jacob's brother, Esau. "Should one brother purchase another as a slave, Lord?" He hated the Edomites as much as he hated the Philistines, and so was vaguely disappointed when he saw fire descended only on the walls of Gaza and not Edom as well. An invading army from the north slaughtered everyone in Gaza and then marched on to Ashkelon. Ekron was the last to fall and lay ruined like Gath.

The last few survivors of the nation that had often oppressed Israel fell, dissolved into dust, and blew away in the wind, leaving only an echo of Philistia's grandeur.

"So be it, Lord!" Amos rejoiced. "So be it."

"Amos!"

He blinked, swayed slightly on the ladder, and grasped hold of a sycamore branch to keep from falling. "What?"

"What? *What,* you say? What's the matter with you, my friend?" Jashobeam, the owner of the grove, stood staring up at him, arms akimbo.

"Nothing."

"Nothing? You've been shouting."

Other workers stared at him.

"I was having a vision."

"Oh, a vision." Jashobeam threw back his head and laughed loudly. He waved his hands as he called out to the others. "Amos was having a vision!"

Some laughed. Some leaned out from beneath branches to grin at him.

Jashobeam put his hands on his hips and looked up at him. "Perhaps you need to come down and rest in the shade awhile. Too much heat, I would say. Go have a long cool drink of water with a little wine."

Face burning, Amos ducked his head. "I'm fine." Clenching his teeth, he grasped another sycamore fig and made the small slice.

"A vision." Jashobeam shook his head. "If you have another, try not to shout about it. You distract my workers." Jashobeam walked away.

✦　✦　✦

Amos was on his way home to Tekoa when the Lord spoke to him again.

The people of Tyre have sinned again and again, and I will not let them go unpunished!

Dropping to his knees, Amos threw himself onto his face.

Israelites stood in the court of the Phoenician king. The heads of state signed documents, swearing a treaty of brotherhood and friendship between Phoenicia and Israel. But then Phoenicians raided, and took whole villages captive to Edom, selling them as slaves.

Amos slammed his fists on the ground. "They tricked us. They broke their word!"

God's wrath descended in a spear of flame that set the great city of Tyre on fire. The mighty fortresses crumbled in the inferno.

There was no respite for Amos this time as a fourth vision came. Edomites with raised swords chased down their Israelite brothers. Every face was like Esau's, filled with bitterness and hatred against his brother Jacob, with generation after generation of them raised on the story of how the younger brother had bought the elder's birthright with a bowl of lentil soup and stripped Esau of his blessing. They sought every opportunity to inflict pain and suffering on Jacob's descendants. They savored revenge like a sweet dessert, not knowing it would turn their souls sour with poison.

Wailing to heaven, Amos gripped his head. "Stop, Lord. I don't want to see any more."

The Edomites caught up with and cut down the fleeing Israelite men. With cries of jubilance and triumph, they stabbed and slashed them, giving free rein to years of pent-up jealousy and rage.

So I will send down fire on Teman, and the fortresses of Bozrah will be destroyed.

Amos watched punishment come upon Esau's sons. The horror of it made him collapse. He spread his arms, clutching the grass, his cheek pressed against soft earth.

✦　✦　✦

He wandered for days, unsure what to do. "Why do You show me these things, Lord? What am I to do with this knowledge? Tell me!"

The Lord did not answer.

Distraught, burdened by the images of destruction, Amos headed again for Tekoa. He climbed the mountain road from Jericho and took shelter for the night in a small cave. He could look out over the Sea of Salt. To the north were the mountains of Ammon. To the south was Moab.

The people of Ammon have sinned again and again, and I will not let them go unpunished!

Terror gripped Amos as he dwelt within the vision. All his senses awakened. He smelled the smoke of Gilead, the burning flesh. He tasted ash in his mouth. Ammonite warriors attacked Gilead. Lungs straining, he ran with the fleeing Israelites. Gilead burned, but even this destruction did not satisfy the Ammonites, who sought to wipe out the race by knocking pregnant women to the ground. As the women screamed for mercy, the warriors ripped their clothing and cut their bellies open with their swords to kill their unborn children.

Amos screamed. "Why do You stand idly by? Why are You silent? Don't You see Your enemies killing Your people?" Tears poured down his cheeks as he raged. "Do to them what You did to Egypt and the Midianites. Crush their pride. Destroy them!"

See what I will do.

Fire descended on Rabbah, blazing through the fortresses until they crumbled. Battle cries rose like a whirlwind in a mighty storm and the Ammonites fell, thousands of them, until only a remnant remained. When the battle ended, the king and his princes were fitted in yokes and led away to slavery.

"Yes, Lord!" Amos raised his hands. "Let all the nations see You are supreme over all the earth!"

Another vision came in the wake of Ammon's destruction.

Moabites opened the graves of Edom's kings and piled up the bones to burn. When the fires grew cold, workers scraped and swept the lime ashes into vats, where they pounded what remained to dust that they used to make plaster. Amos watched in horror and disgust as the Moabites coated their houses with the bones of Edom's kings.

"Not even in death are their victims shown mercy!" Amos shouted.

Before his eyes, an army attacked Moab. Foreign warriors shouted. Rams' horns blew. Flames reached into the sky as Kerioth burned while the people of Moab fell in the noise of battle. Neither their king nor their princes survived the slaughter. Those who had taken the bones of the dead from tombs would never rest in one.

The enemies of Israel would fall. Those who thought they held power would become powerless. God would avenge those who had been skinned alive, those who had been executed, their heads stacked as trophies before the Aramean city gates. No more would Philistia profit on slave trade. No more would Phoenicia break treaties of peace and take whole villages captive into slavery. No more would Edom grow rich on revenge. All of them would die, having drunk the poison of lust and hatred, from Damascus to Ammon and Moab, begun by Lot's incestuous daughters. All of them would be crushed like scorpions beneath the heel of God's anger.

A deep satisfaction had filled Amos at the thought of

their destruction. Exhausted, Amos curled on his side in the shallow cave, comforted. *When, Lord? When will it happen?*

Soon, he hoped. He would relish the sight of it.

✦   ✦   ✦

Amos arose in the morning and offered a prayer of thanksgiving. It was the first he had said—and meant—in years. "Give thanks to the Lord Almighty, for the Lord is compassionate and gracious, slow to anger, abounding in love."

Caravans wound their way up the Benjamin Mountains. Men pulled at roped donkeys laden with packs. As Amos walked up the mountain road, uneasiness filled him. When he reached the Mount of Olives, he stopped and stared, troubled in his soul. He thought again of the corruption he saw every time he went to Jerusalem. Priests like Heled profited off stealing from God. Had Amos not cut his share and built his flock from those same lambs? He shuddered at his guilt. What choice had those priests given his father? Frustrated by helplessness, he tried to make excuses. None sufficed. Words spoken long ago, when he was a child attending classes, came back to him. Burning words that rent his conscience:

"Hear, O Israel. You must love the Lord your God with all your heart, all your soul, and all your strength."

Love had not motivated his rebellion against Heled, nor had righteousness or any desire to worship the Lord. He had not loved God. He had blamed the Lord for the trouble men caused and the contract under which his family lived. Each time he went to the Temple, he did so grudg-

ingly and offered only what was required to keep in good
standing with the authorities.

Uzziah might be king, but all too often it was the priests
who ruled the lives of common people like himself and his
brothers.

The Lord is God!

But even now, as he stood looking up at King David's
Zion, Amos knew idols still pocked Judah's landscape, and
pagan altars still remained despite King Uzziah's attempt
to destroy the foreign gods that had dwelt in the hearts of
King Solomon's wives and concubines. How could a wise
man be so foolish as to build pagan temples and altars?
Amos saw the remnants of those gods as he moved his
flocks. Sometimes he had been tempted to follow the pro-
cessions up those hills so that he could spread himself
beneath the leafy branches and enjoy the sensual pleasures
offered there. It had not been fear of the Lord that kept
him away, but fear of leaving his flock untended.

You must not have any other god but Me. You must
not make for yourself an idol of any kind.

Sin was everywhere. It was in the nations surrounding
Judah and Israel. It was in Israel and Judah.

It was in *him.*

*Not once have I sought out one of the few priests known to
serve in fear of the Lord! I have held my anger close, embrac-
ing it, fanning my hatred against all Your priests. I have
rebelled against You.*

You must not misuse the name of the Lord your God.

Amos cringed. Yes, Heled and others like him were
guilty, but Amos's family had entered into a contract that

dishonored God as well. How many times had they used God's name to seal a bargain?

"Stand aside!" Someone shoved him from behind.

Amos moved out of the way, seeing everything differently.

Remember to observe the Sabbath day by keeping it holy.

Did the gates of Jerusalem not stand open for trade every day of the week? The markets of the great city never rested. Amos watched the beehive of activity as merchants bore their wares into Jerusalem past elders holding court in the gate.

Other commandments came in a rush:

Honor your father and mother. You must not murder. You must not commit adultery. You must not steal. You must not testify falsely against your neighbor. You must not covet your neighbor's house. You must not covet your neighbor's wife, male or female servant, ox or donkey, or anything else that belongs to your neighbor.

Amos closed his eyes. Though he had never broken these commandments in deed, he knew he had broken every one of them in thought.

He had loved his father, but had been bitterly disappointed in him. Not once after he had learned the truth had he believed anything his father said.

And how many times had he lusted for revenge against Heled? He had even thought of ways to kill him, savoring the thought in his mind. If he could have found a way to kill the priest and escape, he might have done it!

From the time he was born until two years ago, he had been a thief, a party to the priests who testified falsely against those who brought perfect offerings to the Lord, only to have them rejected.

As for the sin of coveting, had he not coveted the priests' power, freedom, and wealth? He had not so much wanted it for himself as he had wanted to see it ripped from the hands that had grasped it and held on at such cost to the people.

Amos saw what God wanted him to see and stood mortified by the sins of the people, sins he himself had committed on a daily basis.

And when God spoke, His next words were no surprise.

The people of Judah have sinned again and again, and I will not let them go unpunished! They have rejected the instruction of the Lord, refusing to obey His decrees. They have been led astray by the same lies that deceived their ancestors.

The hair on the back of Amos's neck prickled. He dropped to his knees and covered his face. He rocked forward, covering his head with his hands. "No, Lord, please, don't show me." He drew his knees up under him. "Have mercy on us."

But the images came upon him relentlessly, melting his heart and filling him with a sorrow and compassion he had never felt before when looking upon his own people. The compassion he'd felt until now only for his defenseless sheep. He wept.

"You there. You're blocking us." Hauled up, he was pitched aside and fell heavily. "Stay off the road!"

Heavy wheels crunched the rocks. Oxen blew out their

breath. The voices of a thousand people mingled as Amos sat in the dust, his head in his hands.

"To what end, Lord? To what end will You destroy the people You chose?"

From the ruins I will rebuild it and restore its former glory, so that the rest of humanity, including the Gentiles—all those I have called to be Mine— might seek Me.

✦   ✦   ✦

"What are you doing back so soon?" Bani rose from his money table. When he came close, he frowned. "What's happened? Is Ithai well?"

"I have not seen Ithai or Elkanan in months. Remember, they had finished their business with Joram before I returned with my flock. They came here to Jerusalem before I did."

Ahiam closed the gate of a stall, a lamb in his arms. "The boys went home to Tekoa not long after the new moon festival."

Amos looked at his two brothers. "The Lord spoke to me. I have seen visions."

Ahiam laughed. "Go sleep off the wine over there." He walked away with the lamb.

"You've probably had a fever." Bani searched Amos's face. "You do look ill."

"I have seen the destruction of Jerusalem."

"You're mad. With Uzziah on the throne?" Bani shook his head. "Jerusalem is secure, and our borders are pro-tected."

"But I'm telling you the truth! I saw—"

"Fever-induced dreams, Amos." Bani gripped his arm. "That's all. Besides, why would God speak to you, a shepherd? You're not a member of the priests' guild. You're not a Levite. When God speaks, He talks to one of the trained prophets or priests. Go over there. Sit. You look tired." He led Amos to the bench beneath the canopy where their tables were set up for business.

Amos saw the open box with its neat rows of coin and shuddered.

Bani slapped him on the back. "Have some wine, little brother. Eat something. Forget about whatever you thought you saw. You'll feel better." Bani poured him a cup of wine and offered him bread and dates. "You spend too much time alone with that flock of yours, little brother. You always have."

The hum of conversations merged with the bleating sheep until the sounds seemed the same. Amos clutched his head. *Am I going mad that men are beginning to sound like sheep, or sheep are beginning to sound like men?*

Ahiam returned. "Heled is not pleased to see you, Amos. Joram gave him a bad report when he returned from Tekoa, and Heled hasn't forgotten."

Amos raised his head. "If you don't end your dealings with that thief of a priest, you and your family will suffer for it."

Ahiam's face hardened. "Live your life, Amos, and leave mine in peace." He gave a hard laugh. "If we took your advice, we'd all be living in the hills, half starved and seeing visions."

"Leave him alone, Ahiam."

"He makes trouble for us. Even when he can keep his mouth shut, he allows his contempt to show. Look at him!" Ahiam leaned toward Amos. "You look like a beggar."

"He's given both our sons a start on flocks of their own."

"A lot of good it will do them if he keeps on as he has. Everything we've *all* worked for, for over two generations, will be gone!" He glared at Amos. "It happened before. Remember what Father told you. It can happen again. Don't think it can't." He jerked his head. "You forget who holds the power around here."

Amos rose, shaking with rage. "God holds the power!"

Chin jutting, Ahiam came close enough to stand nose to nose with Amos. "And *He* gave it to *them* to use as *they* will."

Amos stood his ground. "The people of Judah have sinned—"

"All of a sudden, you're the judge?" Ahiam gave him a hard shove. "Go home. Prophesy to your sheep."

"Listen to me," Amos cried out in desperation.

"If you made any sense, I might." Ahiam glanced back over his shoulder. "Send him home." He nodded to Bani. "We've got a business to run here." Turning his back on them, he walked toward a customer looking over the lambs. Smiling, he spread his arms in greeting.

Bani drew Amos aside and spoke quietly. "Go back to my house. A few nights' rest in a good bed and some of my wife's cooking and you'll be yourself again."

Amos knew he would never be the same again. Everywhere he looked, he saw things differently than he had before the Voice had spoken to him.

Dream or no dream, his life had changed forever.

+ + +

Amos left the Temple Mount and its stalls of sacrificial animals, passing tables where money changers stacked shekels and half shekels. He went down to the market square where bellowing camels with tasseled harnesses stood laden with huge packs of merchandise. The animals were lined up behind owners who displayed their wares on woven rugs. The scents of dung and spices mingled while vendors shouted their wares, competing with one another as possible customers wandered the bazaar. Shekels clinked and money boxes slammed shut. Donkeys burdened with bundles were pulled along by hard-faced men, cursing and making threats if others did not make room.

Bludgeoned by sound, Amos sought quieter streets. He wandered along narrow alleys lined with booths. Vendors haggled with customers over prices while competitors called enticements to steal patrons away.

"Good shepherd!" one called to Amos. "Come, come! You need a new pair of sandals. Those look worn through. I will give you a good price."

"I will give you a better price."

"He's a thief. Don't listen to him. I have better—"

"Here! Come look at what I have to offer."

The narrow street widened, and Amos stopped to watch stonemasons working on a new house, a foreman shouting instructions to his crew. A few doors down, a carpenter worked on a cart. Wheels of all sizes lined the wall of his shop. Another man planed a table while his wife showed a bench to a woman with three children.

On another street, metalworkers pounded ingots into utensils while coppersmiths pounded trays. A goldsmith displayed earrings, bracelets, necklaces, and cylinders ready for engraving into family seals. Weavers sold cloths and rugs on another street, while the next was lined with bakers. Amos's stomach clenched with hunger, but he didn't stop. He had no money with which to buy. Distracted, he took dried grain from his scrip to ease the ache in his belly.

He wandered into the valley of cheese makers and back up to the canopied stalls with baskets of barley and wheat, jars of oil and jugs of wine, bins of olives and baskets of early figs. Combs of golden honey dripped into bowls, while nearby another merchant called out balm for sale.

Rug merchants and basket weavers called out to him as he passed. A tentmaker haggled with a customer.

Jerusalem was, indeed, a city of wealth and commerce. The people seemed to want for nothing. What they lacked had little to do with the body and everything to do with the heart and soul. All their strength was spent on what they could hold in their hands.

Pausing, Amos listened to a young man play a lyre for a customer while his father attached strings to a kinnor. The customer pointed to a beautifully carved ten-string nebel displayed alongside a row of bone pipes. The boy picked it up and began to play it. At a signal, the boy handed the instrument to his father. He allowed the customer to hold it, pluck the strings, and stroke the carved wood. Amos picked up some reed pipes and admired them. The lust to own would seal the bargain. He put them down quickly and walked away.

Amos went through a gate and down a pathway. Weary, he sat in the shade of a mustard plant and leaned against a wall. Hyssop grew from between the stones.

Across from him was the Mount of Olives. It was quiet here, quiet enough to think, though pondering what he had just seen was the last thing he wanted to do. He pressed the heels of his hands against his eyes.

"I see sin, Lord." Enticing, tempting, seeming to delight and bring satisfaction. "I see it. I see!"

Pride promised pleasure and security, but would bring despair and death instead.

✦   ✦   ✦

Amos walked home in the moonlight. He went to the fold and entered by the narrow gate, walking quietly among the animals, checking each one. When the sun rose, he would let them out into the south pasture. Soon, it would be time to lead them away from Tekoa. One of the lambs heard his voice and came to him quickly, pressing against his leg. Amos hunkered down. "Yes, I'm home, little one." He rubbed the lamb's face.

Go prophesy to My people Israel.

Confused, Amos stood. "Israel?" He spread his hands, looking up at the sky.

"The northern kingdom, Lord? Samaria?"

Go to Bethel.

Why would God send him to speak to the ten tribes who had broken away from Solomon's son Rehoboam? Hadn't they followed after Jeroboam the son of Nebat, foreman of Solomon's workforce? Why not call one from among the ten rebellious tribes to prophesy to their break-away nation?

"I told my brothers I had seen visions, Lord. They

didn't believe me! They thought I was drunk or suffered delirium."

The lamb bleated. The flock sensed his turbulent emotions and moved, restless, nervous.

"Shhhhh. It's all right, sheep." Amos lifted the lamb. He moved slowly among his animals, speaking softly, soothing their fears. He set the lamb down and moved to the gate. Drawing his reed pipe from his belt, he played whatever sweet melody came to mind. The sheep settled again.

Amos looked up at the stars. Before the visions began, he had believed that God didn't notice him or what he did or thought. Now, he realized God saw and knew everything. Still, Amos didn't understand why God would call a poor shepherd—a simple, ordinary man—to speak the Word of the Lord.

My love is unfailing and everlasting. I will be with you wherever you go.

You love me, and yet You send me north with a message of destruction. Even as he wanted to question, Amos knew why. God had filled him with understanding, and was sending him to call His lambs back from destruction.

Had God ever given a prophet a message the people wanted to hear? a message they welcomed and celebrated? Perhaps Israel would listen this time. Even to a shepherd. Why wouldn't they, when the visions God had given him showed the destruction of enemies that surrounded them? They would celebrate just as he had, before he understood that the sins of Judah were not hidden from God's clear and holy gaze. Wealthy, powerful Israel would gloat even more over the judgment upon the nations, and probably gloat over the destruction of their Judean brothers as well, for then, Samaria would become the city on the mountain.

Or would it?

Solomon's foreman had crowned himself King Jeroboam the First, with dreams of a dynasty to follow. To carry that out, he had abolished the Levitical priesthood and established his own. He had turned the people away from Jerusalem by setting up golden calves for them to worship in Bethel and Dan!

They do all these things, Lord, and yet, Judah *is to be destroyed? How can I say these things? How can I leave my own people and go to them? Judah! What of Judah?*

You will be My prophet in Israel. My Spirit will come upon you, and you will speak the Word of the Lord.

Amos felt the weight of his calling, and went down on his hands and knees to plead with God. "I'm not a city dweller, Lord. You know that. I'm a shepherd. A man of flocks and fields. I hate going to Jerusalem and now you want me to go to Bethel, a place even more corrupt? I've done everything I could to stay away from cities. I can't bear being around so many people. And the noise, the confusion is unbearable to me. I'm just a shepherd."

I am your Shepherd, Amos. Will you obey Me?

Though the words came softly and full of tenderness, Amos knew the course of his life lay in the answer. "I am not worthy."

I have called you by name. You are mine.

"But, Lord, You need someone who will make them listen. You need a powerful speaker. You need someone who knows the Law. You need someone who will know how to persuade them to do what You want." He bowed his head, ashamed. "You need someone who loves them, Lord. And I don't care what happens to them!"

I don't need anyone, My child. I want you. Go to Bethel, Amos. My grace is all you need. I will tell you when to speak and what to say.

Grieving, Amos hung his head. "What about my sheep, Lord? How can I entrust them to hirelings?" He looked up, gulping sobs. "My sheep." Tears ran down his cheeks. "No one loves them as I do."

A quiet breeze blew softly through the winter grass, and God whispered:

Feed My sheep.

+   +   +

Amos slept fitfully at the gate of the sheepfold, wakening before dawn. He sat on the wall and gazed at his animals. He knew the traits and personalities of every one of them. He had saved one from a ledge, another from the attack of a lion, another from floodwaters of a wadi. Some stayed close, never venturing far from the flock, while others were prone to wander. Some learned quickly, while others seem destined to get themselves into trouble with every new pasture. His heart ached because he loved them.

"Feed My sheep," the Lord had said last night as dusk came upon the land.

"Forgive me, Lord, but I care more for these animals than I have ever cared for people. Men take care of them-

selves. They do what they want. Sheep are helpless without a shepherd."

Even as he said the words aloud, he wondered if they
were true. He saw things differently this morning. Maybe
it was the visions of destruction that haunted his
thoughts.

"Feed My sheep."

Were men like sheep? He had always thought of them
as wolves or lions or bears . . . especially priests who could
make life miserable if they so chose, and even tear it apart.
But what of the common people, men and women like him
who wanted to do what was right, but often ended up
doing what was expedient? He had been taught never to
argue with a priest, but his heart had often raged within
him.

He turned toward the north, thinking of Bethel. This
city of the northern kingdom was not that far away—
only eleven miles—but it seemed a distant country. His
journeys had kept him in the pastures of Judah and
Benjamin's territory, always circling him back home to
Tekoa. Bethel was the last place he wanted to go. But he
would have no peace until he obeyed the Lord.

In the cool of the morning, Amos spotted Elkanan
and Ithai as they led their flocks out to pasture. Amos
remained on the wall of his fold, watching his nephews
with the flocks he had started for them. What he saw
pleased him. Stepping down, Amos opened the gate and
led his sheep out. Elkanan and Ithai saw him and raised
their hands in greeting. Amos headed toward them.

Elkanan greeted him warmly. "Uncle!"

As soon as Elkanan withdrew, Ithai embraced him as

well. "You spend less time in Jerusalem each year." Ithai laughed.

Jerusalem. Sorrow gripped Amos as the vision came flooding back. *Jerusalem!* How long had he despaired at what he saw there. Never had he felt such a wave of sorrow as he did now with dark wrenching memories of the future.

He stayed with his nephews for the rest of the day, listening to their stories of predators thwarted, sick lambs tended, wandering sheep found, sheepfolds expanded to accommodate more animals. Amos understood. Rather than go out alone with their flocks, they had stayed together, sharing the burden of tending the sheep.

His moment came to speak. "I have been called away."

Elkanan glanced at him. "Away? When? Where?"

"Before sunrise tomorrow." He leaned heavily on his staff and swallowed the lump in his throat. "Add my flock to yours and tend them as I would."

Elkanan looked at the sheep and then at Amos. "Should we stay here in Tekoa until you return, Uncle?"

"No. Take them to fresh pastures. The pastures of Jericho are open to you. If Jashobeam questions you, tell him these are my sheep. I paid for grazing rights by working in his sycamore groves. If I have not returned by the time you come back here to winter the flocks, take only the *best* lambs to Jerusalem."

His pulse raced suddenly, as he remembered the Lord roaring like a lion inside his head. "Whatever you do, do it as the Lord would have you do it. Do what is right, no matter what others do. Run from evil."

Elkanan stared. "What's happened, Uncle?"

"The Lord has shown me what will happen to us if
we don't repent and turn back to Him."

A flood of questions came from his nephews. Amos
found solace that they did not suggest he rest. They did
not tell him to eat something so that he would feel like
himself again. "Sin brings death, my sons. Do what is
right. Convince your fathers of this. God sees what men
do. He knows their hearts. Do what is right and live."

"We will tell them, Uncle."

They seemed troubled. Even if they could be convinced, would Ahiam and Bani listen? Amos doubted it.
Bani might consider turning away from the business prac-
tices that had made him prosper, but not for long. Ahiam
would wear him down and turn him back to worshiping
profits. Amos remembered how his father's conscience had
suffered. But Ahiam and Bani had lived most of their lives
in the shadow of the Temple among corrupt priests that
saw nothing wrong with what they did. Now, they
equated their increasing wealth to God's blessing on
what they did.

"Uncle? Why are you crying?"

Amos struggled against the emotions overwhelming
him, and tried to keep his voice steady. "I must go to
Bethel." He headed across the field.

"Bethel! But, Uncle . . . how long will you be gone?"

"I don't know." *A few weeks, Lord? A month? A year?*
Silence.

Maybe it was better not to know.

AMOS camped in the hills near Bethel. He could see lamp-light on the wall and knew soldiers were stationed in the watchtowers.

Bethel! After stealing Esau's birthright, Jacob had fled and stopped to rest here, using a stone for a pillow. In his vision, he saw a ladder to heaven with angels going up and down, and God had made a covenant with him. No wonder Jeroboam I had claimed this city to start his new religion. Even having been delivered from Egypt, the Israelites had quickly returned to the pagan worship of their oppressors while Moses was on top of Mount Sinai receiving the Law of God. Jeroboam had seduced the ten northern tribes with the same god—a golden calf. And the people wanted convenience. Why walk eleven miles to Jerusalem to worship the true God three times a year, when there was another god right here in Bethel? Jeroboam had known the people well. He gave them what they wanted: empty idols made by human hands and the illusion of control over their own lives.

Jeroboam, a goat leading the sheep to slaughter. He knew what places meant the most to the people and claimed them. Another golden calf resided in Gilgal where the Israelites had crossed the Jordan River after forty years of wandering in the wilderness. Gilgal, the place where the people of Israel had reconsecrated themselves to God and celebrated the first Passover in Canaan; the place where they had eaten the first fruit of the land after forty years of manna. And now it, too, stood defiled by pagan worship. Even Beer-sheba, where God first made promises of blessing to

Abraham, then Isaac, and finally Jacob, was now a major place of worship for Jeroboam's unholy religion.

Amos slept uneasily and awakened in darkness. He rose and went down the hill to the road and followed it up to the gates of Bethel where he waited until morning. Merchants arrived with their goods, ignoring the beggars who approached them. Some of the poor had little more than a tunic to keep them warm. When the gates were opened, Amos tensely moved among the crowds making their way to the center of the city where Jeroboam's temple stood, housing the golden calf.

The mount was an anthill of activity with pilgrims carrying their offerings up and into the temple. Neophyte priests dressed in fine linen ephods stood greeting them as they entered. Not one Levite stood among them, for Jeroboam I had abolished the rightful priesthood and established his own. All a man needed to become a priest was one young bull and seven rams! And who with the means would not pay it when all the benefits of priesthood could so enrich a man and his family? Power, wealth, and prestige came with the post, and the ability to strip the people of whatever they decided was a "proper offering" to stay in the good graces of Jeroboam's false and capricious gods.

Having driven even the faithful Levites from the northern cities, no one remained to teach people the truth.

"Alms for the blind . . . ," a man whined at the bottom of the steps, a small woven basket in his hand. He held it out at the sound of people passing. "Alms for the blind. Have pity on me."

Amos paused to look into his face. The man's eyes were opaque, his face brown and lined from years in the sun. He was clothed in rags, and his gnarled hands revealed that blindness was not his only infirmity. Amos had brought only a few shekels with him. He took one from his pouch and leaned down. "May the Lord have compassion on you." Amos placed the coin in the basket.

The man's fingers fumbled over the coin as he declared his thanks.

As Amos went up the steps, he watched priests take gifts of money and tuck them into their personal purses. One put his hand out as Amos came level with him. Amos looked at him in contempt.

The priest stiffened. "Those who do not give to god cannot expect blessing."

"I will not receive a blessing from your god." Amos started to walk by.

"Indeed not if you are so ungracious and ungrateful. You will have a curse on your head. . . ."

Pausing, Amos turned and gazed deeply into the man's eyes. "Woe to you, false priest. You already live under a curse of your own making." Turning his back on him, Amos walked into the temple.

He moved with the others, watchful, taking in everything. Were men so eager to be fleeced? Amos went as far as the inner corridor and stood aside. Leaning on his staff, he watched and listened to men and women murmuring incoherently as they moved forward, intent upon seeing the golden calf in which they placed their hope. Some carried small woven prayer rugs that they unrolled and knelt upon in comfort. They raised their hands and bowed in adoration before the horned altar. They sang songs of praise. Priests waved incense burners. The streaks of cloying gray smoke made a cloud over the worshipers held there by a fog of lies.

And there stood their god in all its glory. Did these people really believe that bloodless empty statue could answer prayers?

So it seemed.

These Israelite brothers no longer knew the difference between righteousness and blasphemy. How was it possible to put such ardent faith in that great hunk of hollow gold, molded and shaped by a man? That calf couldn't help itself, let alone do anything for them! Men without God put their trust in a spider's web, not even knowing they had been captured and bound. Everything these people counted upon to keep them safe would fall, pulling them down with it.

Musicians strummed lyres and kinnors. Priests chanted.

A woman rushed tearfully to her husband, displaying a talisman sold to her by a priest. "He says we will have a child. . . ."

A man, sallow and gaunt, had paid for a spell to be cast so that he would be healed of his troubles.

Amos followed a father and son out of the temple. "I've already put in my request, Son. You will be well pleased with the one I have chosen. Since it is your birthday, you will go first, and I will wait my turn."

When they went into another building next door, Amos followed. As he entered the door, he heard laughter. Men and women lounged in a room off to his right. Someone strummed a lyre.

A girl dressed in finery, her dark eyes made up with Egyptian kohl, rose to greet him. Her smile did not reach her eyes. "Come with me." Bells tinkled as she walked.

Amos didn't move. "What is this place?"

She turned and stared at him. "The temple brothel."

When her expression became curious, it was the first sign of life in her face. "Do you prefer boys?"

"Boys?"

She shrugged. "Some do."

Amos left the house quickly. He crossed the courtyard and stood in the shadows of a temple wall. A vision came back: the screams of the dying, the smoke, bodies sprawled in the streets. Leaning heavily on his staff, he bowed his head. *Now, Lord? Do I speak now?*

God did not answer.

Amos sat on the temple steps and waited. All around him, people hurried to sin, laughing as they went. The wealthy pushed past the impoverished. If they paused at all, it was to mock rather than show pity.

How had Israel sunk to this? Did it go back to the days of Solomon when that great king of supposed wisdom had allowed his wives and concubines to turn his heart from God? The Lord had used the foreman of Solomon's workforce to break the kingdom in two. The king's spies had told him a prophet foretold Jeroboam as ruler over ten of the twelve tribes. Rather than heed God's warning and repent, Solomon attempted to kill Jeroboam.

Escaping to Egypt, Jeroboam waited until the king's death and then returned to make his move for power. He asked Rehoboam, Solomon's son, now king, to lighten the workload upon the people.

God knew the pride of men, but still gave them opportunity to repent. Wise counselors surrounded Rehoboam and gave him sound advice. Rehoboam refused to listen, preferring instead the witless counsel of spoiled, arrogant young men who told him he would be greater even than the great King Solomon.

King Solomon had loved women more than God. His desire to please them led the people astray, for one wife wanted an altar for the pagan god Chemosh, another bowed down to the detestable idol of Moab, and others worshiped Molech, the idol of Ammon, on the mountain east of Jerusalem. Solomon was even led to worship Ashtoreth, the goddess of the Sidonians, and Milcom of the Ammonites.

How could a man reputed to be the wisest on earth have been so foolish?

King Rehoboam attempted to show his authority by sending a servant to call the people back to work. When the servant was stoned to death, Rehoboam fled to Jerusalem. He rallied the tribes of Judah and Benjamin and called up warriors to go to war, but the Lord sent word through His prophet to stop what he was doing. "Do not go to war against your brothers!" This time, Rehoboam listened and repented. Any man who fought against God was destined to lose, and he wanted to retain the power he had. He stayed in Jerusalem and ruled over Judah and Benjamin, expecting the other ten tribes to return. After all, the Lord required them to come three times a year to Jerusalem to worship, and the Levites would draw them back to God— and to the rightful king.

Jeroboam knew the risks. He had no trust in God even though the Lord had given him the ten tribes. He made his own plans and gave the Israelites the god their ancestors had worshiped in Egypt—a golden calf. Hadn't the tribes wanted to return to Egypt? Hadn't they always been tempted to follow the ways of the other nations? Even Aaron, brother of the great lawgiver Moses, had made a golden calf. Jeroboam gave them two and placed them in

cities where God had spoken to the patriarchs—Bethel and
Dan.

"Here are your gods, Israel!"

The people rejoiced and flocked to worship the golden
calves.

Jeroboam's religion grew so rapidly and prospered so
greatly he set up golden calves and goats in Gilgal and
Beersheba. He built palaces on "watch mountain,"
Samaria, his capital. Shrines sprung up like poisonous
plants throughout the territories. He silenced all protests
by abolishing the Levitical priesthood established by God.
The new priesthood did as the king wanted, raking in pro-
ceeds from the royal sanctuaries.

Jeroboam's cunning plan worked. Men wanted ease,
after all, not hard work. Ah, yes, why not worship idols?
A man would have immediate pleasure with temple prostitutes. Sin would be approved. No one need consider what
is right or wrong. Live for yourselves. Go ahead: lie, cheat,
steal—everyone is doing it—as long as you give the king
his share of the offerings! Why serve a holy God who
demanded you follow the Law, when other gods would
allow you to wallow in self-gratification? People rejected
truth and gulped down lies, turning their backs on the
loving, merciful God who provided their every need.
Instead, they followed a king who ruled over them as he
pleased.

*Shall I speak here, Lord? Shall I speak now against all
I see?*

Still, God did not answer.

Frustration filled Amos. His anger grew the longer he
waited. Sin stood upon the altar, and the people praised it!
Bethel, once a holy place, now a city of blasphemy! He

could not bear to listen to the priests calling the people into that foul temple for worship. Turning away, he pushed through the crowd. "Let me through!" he cried out, eager to make his way off the temple mount and down the thronged street.

Only after he left the city behind did he feel he could breathe again.

He gave a cry of pent-up emotion and went out into the hills. Jerusalem was bad enough, but now he saw this place! He spread his arms and roared, "Israel! Israel!" The ten tribes wallowed in sin and did not even recognize it. He paced and circled, muttering to himself. Finally, he sank down and tried to plead. "Lord . . . Lord . . ."

A glorious sunset crossed the western sky. The tinkle of bells made him raise his head. A shepherd led his sheep across a field toward home.

Amos held his head in his hands. "Send me home, Lord. Let me prophesy to Your people in Judah and Benjamin. Please, Lord."

No answer came.

Amos wept.

✦   ✦   ✦

Amos wandered the city of Bethel each day, waiting for the Lord to tell him to speak. On the temple mount, he smelled the stench of incense the priests offered, heard their chants and songs. Along streets and in markets, the wealthy used their power to take whatever they wanted from lesser people, parading their finery and privilege before those they cheated.

Sometimes he'd stand in the shadows of a gate and listen to the elders turn laws to their own favor and strip the

poor of what little they had. One judge took the robe from
a poor man and handed it over to a merchant for a jug of
wine. Another took an unfortunate's sandals as pledge for
a debt, and had not even a grimace of guilt as the man
hobbled away to work in a rock quarry.

Shaking with rage, Amos turned away and headed up
the hill. He heard shouts of greeting and looked back. A
delegation approached.

Holy fire poured into Amos's veins as God spoke to
him. He strode down the hill and extended his staff, pointing at them as the Lord spoke through him. "This is what
the Lord says: 'The people of Damascus have sinned again
and again, and I will not let them go unpunished!'"

Amos's voice rose above the din of the crowd, echoing
in the narrow street. "'They beat down My people in
Gilead as grain is threshed with iron sledges. So I will send
down fire on King Hazael's palace, and the fortresses of
King Ben-hadad will be destroyed. I will break down the
gates of Damascus and slaughter the people in the valley of
Aven. I will destroy the ruler in Beth-eden, and the people
of Aram will go as captives to Kir,' says the Lord."

"Who is this beggar who speaks insults?" Faces red
with consternation, the Assyrians protested loudly. "Is
this the way Ben-hadad's servants are greeted when they
come in peace?"

Amos came on. "You speak of peace, but war is in your
hearts."

"Be careful what you say. You may find your head on
a pole!"

"Go back to Damascus!"

The people moved away from Amos, staring, as he cried

out, "Go and tell your king what the Lord God has said!
Get out of here!"

People whispered and then began talking. Some called
out. Soon, the street was full as people surrounded Amos.
Heart pounding, he shouted and raised his staff again. The
people let him pass as he strode down the street. He was
eager to get away from this place, away from them.

They called out questions. He didn't answer.

"Who is he?"

"I don't know."

"He looks like a shepherd."

"But did you hear him speak!"

"Just a madman talking."

"I've never heard a man speak with such authority.
Have you?"

The Lord's judgment excited them. Hadn't he felt the
same? *"Let it come, Lord! Let it come."*

People shouted from all directions.

"Did you hear what the prophet said?"

"Damascus in ruins!"

"That's a sight I'd like to see."

When it had to do with judgment upon their enemies,
why wouldn't they celebrate? Why not cheer and shout?
The Lord had given them words to savor, visions to
delight. They listened to His Words.

Would they keep listening?

Amos ducked down a side street.

"Where is he going?"

"Prophet! Wait! Give us another prophecy."

Amos remembered other visions the Lord had shown
him and ran. Now was not the time. He must wait upon
the Lord. He must wait! Some gave chase. Turning down

another street and then another, Amos left them behind. Out of breath, his body shook violently. Emotions warred within him—wrath that made him grind his teeth and groan, anguish that brought a torrent of tears. "Lord, *Lord*!"

The wave of emotion crested and ebbed, leaving him drained. He sank against the wall, squatting on his heels. His staff clattered to the packed ground. Still panting, he rested his arms on his raised knees and bowed his head.

A door opened, and a woman stood staring at him. When he met her gaze, she stepped inside and closed the door.

Children played in the street.

A bird chirped from a sprig of hyssop growing from a high wall.

A man and woman argued across the way.

Tensing at the sound of running feet, Amos stood. Shouts and curses. Excited laughter. Youths ran past. One spilled a few coins. Their sandals echoed as an angry man came tearing around the corner, pausing long enough to snatch up the dropped coins and take after them again.

A lattice window opened above him. Amos looked up as a woman leaned out. Dressed in an expensive Babylonian robe, she sipped from a silver goblet. "What are you doing down there?" Not waiting for an answer, she disappeared and a servant appeared at the window and dumped a bowlful of something. Amos barely managed to evade being covered by household slops. The wealthy woman leaned out again and laughed at him.

Amos found his way to the main gate. A man recognized him and whispered to the elders. He did not stay long enough for anyone to detain him.

✦   ✦   ✦

Amos found a small cave in the hills where he could spend
the night. The next morning, he waited and prayed until
God impelled him to return to Bethel where, as soon as he
entered the gate, he heard the buzz of whispers.

"He's back! The prophet is back."

A young man pressed through the crowd and ran up
the street. No one tried to stop Amos or ask questions
when he passed through the gate and entered into the
city. People followed him to the temple mount and then
stood watching, talking behind their hands to one
another, eyes eager. He sat on the lowest step of the temple and waited. Someone put a plate down in front of him,
and people began putting coins into it. Angry, he kicked
it away. With a collective gasp, they drew back and
stared. Some quickly retrieved the coins they had offered.

"The priests are coming. . . ."

"The priests . . ."

The young man who had run from the gate came down
the steps with two priests. Amos did not stand for them.
They murmured to one another and then stood between
him and the people.

The taller priest spoke quietly. "You stirred the people
yesterday with your prophecy against Damascus."

Some people edged closer, faces rapt and eager.

Amos looked from them to the priests. He rested his
staff across his knees. "These people are easily stirred."

"We would like to talk with you, Prophet, hear what
you have to say." The tall priest glanced pointedly toward
the men and women closing in. "Perhaps you prefer somewhere more private."

"Ask what you will here and now, though I probably will not be able to answer."

"What is your name?"

"Amos." He had never given much thought to his name, but now he wondered if God had caused his parents to give it to him: "burden bearer." His heart was truly burdened with the task God had given him, burdened even more by the visions he carried in his mind.

"And your village?"

"Tekoa."

People whispered, murmured.

"You are Judean."

"Yes, and God has called me here to speak His Word."

"What else would God have you say to us?"

"I speak in His time, not mine."

"Your prophecy against Damascus is well received. We all gave thanks to God yesterday. We would have invited you to speak again, but you disappeared. Where did you go?"

"Out into the hills."

"You should have shelter."

"The Lord is my shelter."

"Come, Prophet. Join us inside the temple. We have room for you here. We will worship together."

Heat filled Amos's face. He had no intention of being drawn inside that vile place. "I will come and sit here and wait upon the Lord."

Dark eyes glinted, smooth words were murmured. "As you wish." They bowed in respect and went back up the steps. The man who had reported Amos's arrival remained outside. He insinuated himself among the watchers. Two

temple guards came down and took positions. Amos
smiled faintly.

The morning passed slowly. People drifted away. When
Amos was thirsty, he lifted his skin of water to his lips.
When he was hungry, he took grain and raisins from his
scrip.

The guards sought shade. Others came to take their
place.

Amos left as the sun was setting, but he returned the
next day and the next, and the next after that. His tongue
felt like a weight in his mouth. Day after day, he watched
the people of Bethel live their lives, cheat one another,
seek the solace of prostitutes, and give their offerings to
idols. He waited and prayed. And people forgot about
him.

When he came one morning, Philistines stood in the
gate. Backs straight, heads high, they spoke to the elders
who deferred to them nervously.

Fire flooded Amos's blood, and the quickening of the
Holy Spirit took hold.

"This is what the Lord says." He strode toward them.
"The people of Gaza have sinned again and again, and
I will not let them go unpunished! They sent whole villages into exile, selling them as slaves to Edom. So I will
send down fire on the walls of Gaza, and all its fortresses
will be destroyed."

Fury spread across the faces of the Philistines. Two
drew swords.

Amos blocked one with his club and used his staff to
yank the other man around and pitch him to the ground.
Swords clattered on the stones. When the fallen warrior

tried to rise, Amos slammed his heel on his back. He sent the other crashing against a wall.

"*This is what the Lord says!*" His voice thundered in the gate. "I will slaughter the people of Ashdod and destroy the king of Ashkelon. Then I will turn to attack Ekron, and the few Philistines still left will be killed." He lifted his foot and stepped back so the fallen man could scramble to his feet. "Go back!" He drove them from the gate. "Go and take the Word of the Lord with you to your king."

Pandemonium reigned. A crowd surrounded Amos. People pressed in upon him from all sides. Strangely, he felt no fear, no desire to run away again. Even as he was swept along like a leaf on a stream, he felt calm. The temple of Bethel loomed before him, a gathering of priests waiting. Guards poured down the steps and took Amos into custody while the priests calmed the crowd.

One priest came close and put his hand upon Amos's arm. "You bring us good news."

Amos withdrew his arm. "I speak the Word of the Lord."

The priest's eyes grew cold, calculating, searching. "As do we."

Another beckoned. "You must have lodgings within the city."

Amos held his staff in front of him. "I have lived my life in the fields of the Lord."

"A man of your importance should live in comfort."

Someone tugged Amos's sleeve. "I can give you lodgings."

"No! Come with me."

"I have a summer house you can stay in!"

Surprised by such offers, Amos turned to the people.

"The Lord has provided me with a place to live." He headed down the steps.

"Prophet!" one of the priests called out. "Will you give us no answer?"

Amos regarded the group in their finery. "God will answer you." Turning, he headed across the courtyard. People clustered around him, asking questions, praising him, pleading for another prophecy. They crowded so close to him, he could scarcely move.

"Let him pass!" a priest shouted.

The people retreated enough so he could proceed toward the street leading to the main gate. Guards appeared, and the people quieted. Amos breathed in relief when he left the confines of Bethel. Glancing back, he saw a group of men following him and tried to send them away.

"We just want to talk with you!"

Flustered, needing solitude, Amos headed for the hills. He walked in a seemingly aimless pattern, knowing the city dwellers would grow tired and give up. When the sun began to set, Amos went to the small cave in a hillside where he had left his supplies, and settled down for the night.

Voices whispered outside.

"Why does he live in a cave when he could have a room near the temple?"

"I don't know."

Amos pulled his robe up over his head.

Foxes had holes, but it seemed a prophet of the Lord would have no place private to lay his head.

✦   ✦   ✦

When Amos arose, he found gifts at the mouth of his cave. The first day, there was a small basket of fruit. The second, he found a pouch of roasted grain and a woven coat. He awakened to clinking the third day and came outside to find a bowl and offering of coins. Amos took the tunic and coins with him to Bethel. A man in a worn tunic shivered, waiting for the gate to open. Amos tapped him on the shoulder. When the man turned, Amos held out the coat. "This will keep you warm."

The man's eyes narrowed. "Do you mock me? I can't afford such a coat."

"I'm giving it to you."

The man stared at him in surprise and then looked at the coat with longing. Still, he did not raise his hand to take it.

"What's your name?"

"Issachar."

"Why will you not accept the coat, Issachar? You have need of it."

Issachar became angry. "As soon as I show my face inside the gate, I'll be accused of stealing it. I've lost everything. I'd like to keep from having my hand cut off."

"I'll make it clear you came by it honestly."

"And who are you to speak for me? A stranger. I'll still lose it."

"Why?"

"There are those who would take it from me as payment for a debt."

"Only for a day and then, by law, they must return it."

Issachar gave a snort of disdain. "No such law prevails here."

"How much do you owe?"

Issachar told him, and the amount was far less than the

offering that had been left in the basket outside Amos's cave. "Take it." Amos stood beside him. "We will settle your debt when the gate opens."

As he walked the streets, he gave a coin to a man without sandals, and another to an aging Nazirite. While buying what he needed in the marketplace, he saw a widow with four children begging for bread. He gave her the rest of what he had and told her to thank God for the provisions.

Each day, he found more gifts left outside his cave dwelling.

The people showed generosity to him, a stranger, and remained blind to the poor of their city. They liked what he had said. They wanted more favorable prophecies and thought these bribes would keep them coming. It did not occur to them that the Word of the Lord was not for hire.

Amos marveled at how God used their attempts to control prophecy to provide for him and even bless a few of the forgotten and impoverished in Bethel.

Still, Amos knew the time was coming when these gift givers and flatterers would turn against him.

"When will you speak again, Prophet?" an official called out as he entered Bethel one day.

"When God gives me the words."

After a while, no one paid attention to him when he entered Bethel. Even the beggars left him alone, quickly aware that the gifts had stopped and they would receive nothing from his hand. Amos wandered and observed, waiting upon the Lord in the midst of the crowd, thankful he was no longer the center of attention.

He knew it was the calm before the storm.

He spent long hours walking the hills, squatting on his

heels or sitting on a boulder to watch the shepherds with their flocks. He was more at home alone than among the well-dressed, well-fed, prosperous crowds.

One day, he walked long enough and far enough that he could see Tekoa. His heart squeezed tight with pain. Leaning on his staff, he pleaded. "Why must I wait, Lord? Why can I not speak all the visions at once and have done with them?" He felt the answer in his soul and bowed his head.

Oh, that he should care so little about people whom God loved so much.

The sun set. Darkness came. Amos looked up and imagined the hand of God flinging stars like shining dust across the heavens. No. He was wrong to think such pagan thoughts, for God had only to utter a word and it was done. Only man had He shaped with His hands, using dust He created to form His most precious and amazing creation. Only man was molded and loved into being, the breath of life in his lungs given by God.

The canopy of night soothed Amos. He felt God's presence over him. Surely his ancestors had felt the same as they wandered in the wilderness with the cloud by day and pillar of fire by night. God might be silent, but He was near—oh, so near—only a breath away. Burdened with the task God had given him, Amos also felt cherished. Wayward, stubborn, contentious as he was, God loved him.

Did He not also love the people of Bethel and Dan, Gilgal, and Beersheba? Wayward, stubborn, sinful though they were?

"Feed My sheep," God had said.

"Help me see them through Your eyes, Lord. Let me feel

what You feel toward Your people so that I might better serve You."

And suddenly he did. Anguish, rage, passion. A father grieving over a wayward son, crying out to him to *come back to me where you are safe, come back*. . . . Judgment thrown down as a hedge to keep that son from plunging over a precipice straight into the arms of death.

Do you not see? Do you not know? I am your salvation.

Amos dropped to one knee, clutching his staff, swaying with the force of emotions. He moaned. "Lord, Lord . . ."

God had called him to be a prophet, and with each day, he surrendered more. For in those moments when the Spirit of the Lord came upon him, he was *alive*. It was only later when the Lord departed from him that Amos felt the loneliness of his soul. No longer was it enough to know God existed: God heard, saw, and knew him. Amos ached to have God remain indwelled, transforming his mind and heart. He wanted the intimacy to last.

He thought of Elijah taken up to heaven in the flaming chariot, never tasting death, standing now in the presence of the Lord; of Elisha, parting the Jordan River, raising a dead boy. And of Jonah running and hiding, only to be found and made more useful despite his disobedience. Who could doubt the word of a man half digested and vomited on the beach by a fish? Even the hated Assyrians in Nineveh had listened and repented!

For a while anyway.

Amos closed his eyes. "These are Your people, Lord, Your wandering children. You are my Shepherd. Lead me,

Lord, so that I might lead them away from death. Help me."

He would speak the Word of the Lord. But would they come to God's call upon their hearts and minds?

He already feared he knew the answer. Had not the Lord already shown him what would happen?

How soon men forget the Word of the Lord.

And choose to perish in the midst of God's patience.

✦   ✦   ✦

Amos watched a caravan make its way up the hill toward Bethel. His vision blurred, and he saw siege machines, warriors attacking, smoke and fire. He heard screams of terror and pain.

Surging to his feet, he cried out in a loud voice and strode through the orchard. He came out onto the road and raised his staff. "This is what the Lord says: 'The people of Tyre have sinned again and again, and I will not let them go unpunished!'"

Camel jockeys shouted profanities at him.

"They broke their treaty of brotherhood with Israel, selling whole villages as slaves to Edom. So I will send down fire on the walls of Tyre, and all its fortresses will be destroyed."

Animals bayed and paced. Attendants ran back and forth, trying to keep them in line.

Amos ran and placed himself between the caravan and the city. He pointed his staff toward Edom.

"This is what the Lord says: 'The people of Edom have sinned again and again, and I will not let them go unpunished!'"

Visitors backed away from him as he cried out.

"They chased down their relatives, the Israelites, with swords, showing them no mercy. In their rage, they slashed them continually and were unrelenting in their anger."

People lined the walls of Bethel.

"The prophet! The prophet of the Lord speaks!"

"From your mouth to God's ears!"

"This is what the Lord says." Amos pointed his staff toward Ammon. "The people of Ammon have sinned again and again, and I will not let them go unpunished! When they attacked Gilead to extend their borders, they ripped open pregnant women with their swords. So I will send down fire on the walls of Rabbah, and all its fortresses will be destroyed. The battle will come upon them with shouts, like a whirlwind in a mighty storm. And their king and his princes will go into exile together!"

Amos's lungs filled. His heart rose. He entered the gates, his voice like thunder echoing down the streets.

"This is what the Lord says: 'The people of Moab have sinned again and again, and I will not let them go unpunished! They desecrated the bones of Edom's king, burning them to ashes. So I will send down fire on the land of Moab, and all the fortresses in Kerioth will be destroyed. The people will fall in the noise of battle, as the warriors shout and the ram's horn sounds. And I will destroy their king and slaughter all their princes.'"

"The Lord defends Israel!" men shouted.

"Israel is great!"

Blood on fire with the Spirit of the Lord, Amos came outside the gates once again and cried out against Judah. "This is what the Lord says." Tears filled his eyes and sorrow, his voice. "The people of Judah have sinned again and again, and I will not let them go unpunished! They have rejected the instruction of the Lord, refusing to obey His decrees. They have been led astray by the same lies that deceived their ancestors. So I will send down fire on Judah, and all the fortresses of Jerusalem will be destroyed." His voice broke.

The Spirit of the Lord lifted. Amos's blood cooled. He heard people cheering, shouting from the top of the wall. "Bring on the Day of the Lord!" People rushed from Bethel and clustered around him, their voices like chattering birds. "Let it come! Let it come!"

Only a few appeared to be troubled that the Lord's judgment had fallen so close to home.

Is it time, Lord? I have given every prophecy but one. Is it time, Lord?

Wait.

The crowd parted as several priests came toward him. The eldest spoke with cool respect. "Your prophecies please the people." Tightly spoken words, eyes ablaze with jealousy.

"I speak the Word of the Lord."

"So we have been told. And it is true you speak with great power, Amos of Tekoa."

People talked among themselves. "He prophesies against his own country. . . ."

Amos turned away.

The priest quickly caught up with him. "Come." A command.

Amos ignored it.

The priest spoke with less force. "We will reward you for your words."

Amos pressed his way through the throng of people and kept walking.

"Where is he going?"

The priest's voice rose above the din. "We want to hear more of what you have to say to us."

Angry, Amos faced him. "You hear, but you do not understand."

People whispered. "What don't we understand?"

"Shhh. Let him speak."

"Stop shoving!"

"What does he say?"

"Let the Day of the Lord come," the priest called out. "It's what we wait for. We are ready for it!"

Others called out in agreement.

Amos looked up at the wall lined with people. "The Day of the Lord will not be as you imagine."

The people fell silent.

Unable to say more, Amos walked away.

Ducking into the orchard where he had sat all morning, he ran.

✦   ✦   ✦

Sitting in his cave, Amos pressed the heels of his hands against his eyes. *Judah!* His throat tightened. *Judah!*

"Prophet?" Someone stood outside, a dark silhouette against the setting sun. "May I speak with you?"

"Go away!"

"Please." A young voice, broken, questing. "I have to know. Is this judgment upon Judah certain, or will God show mercy upon us?"

Us?

Shuddering, vision blurred by tears, Amos rose. When

the young man bowed before him, he shouted, "Get off
your knees! Am I God that you would bow down to me?"

The young man scrambled to his feet and flinched as
though expecting a blow. "You are the Lord's messenger!"

Shoulders sagging, Amos let out a long sigh, sat, and
rested his staff across his knees. "Unwilling messenger."
He scowled at the intruder. "What do you want?"

"Judah *will* be destroyed, or *may* be destroyed?"

Amos struggled with emotion. "If the people repent,
perhaps the Lord will show mercy on us." Amos held out
little hope of that happening. Only an invading army
seemed to turn men's hearts back to God.

"I have family in Judah. Uncles, aunts, cousins."

"I have brothers." He saw something in the young
man's face that made him soften. "Why are you here?
What do you want of me?"

"You are the Lord's prophet. I want to know. Will not
the Lord hear your prayers?"

"The Lord hears, but so far the Lord had said no to
everything I've asked of Him. Better if you tell your
uncles, aunts, and cousins to *repent*. Tell them to return to
the Lord. Prod them. Plead with them. Pray they will listen!"

The young man looked toward Bethel. "The people of
Bethel hang on your every word. They love what you
have to say."

Amos leaned back, depressed. "Yes. They do, don't
they?" Because every word that had come from his mouth
thus far had proclaimed destruction on their enemies—
or competitors.

"Is there no hope for Judah?"

"I told you. *Repent!* And why are you here in Bethel if you are a Judean?"

"I'm a Levite."

"All faithful Levites returned to Judah long ago."

The young man held his gaze. "Some felt impelled to return here."

"Impelled by God, or self-interest?"

Troubled, the young man bowed his head and didn't answer.

"Afraid to answer?"

The lad's eyes were awash with tears. "In truth, I don't know." He stood and walked away, shoulders slumped.

Amos went into his cave, sank down, and put his head in his hands.

+   +   +

The Lord told Amos to return to Bethel and repeat the prophecies about the surrounding nations. Amos went, calling out as he entered the city. Crowds gathered eagerly to hear him. The young Levite stood in their midst. Unlike those around him who cheered, he listened intently, troubled rather than jubilant. He didn't approach Amos again.

Gifts continued to pile up outside the entrance of Amos's cave. He thanked God for the provisions and gave away everything but the little food he needed.

Each day, Amos preached on the steps of Bethel's temple. "Those who oppress the poor insult their Maker, but helping the poor honors Him."

The people listened, but did not apply the words to their own lives. Even the priests thought he spoke only of the surrounding nations and Judah to the south.

"Fools make fun of guilt, but the godly acknowledge it

and seek reconciliation with God! Godliness makes a nation great, but sin is a disgrace to any people."

The people clapped at his preaching, nodding and smiling to one another. Was there any nation as religious as Israel? Fervent in worship, they flocked to the temples and shrines, singing and dancing. They poured out offerings. Puffed up with pride and prosperity, they grew smug and self-righteous. *Look at us! Look at the evidence of our righteousness!*

They had gold in abundance and an army ready to defend them. King Jeroboam II lived in splendor in the capital of Samaria, having succeeded in pushing back the borders to what they had been during the reign of the great King Solomon. Such blessing had to be a sign of God's approval.

Amos knew better. He preached on the sins of the nations, but no one saw any similarity to the way they thought and lived. They continued to look at the nations around them, rather than into their own hearts.

The trap was set . . . and would soon be sprung.

✦ ✦ ✦

One afternoon Amos again found the young Levite waiting outside his cave, along with several others. He stood as Amos approached. "May I speak with you?" He spoke more softly. "In private?"

Amos sent the others away. Leaning on his staff, he looked at the young man. "You have not returned to Jerusalem."

"I spent a week with my relatives in Jerusalem. I told them everything you said."

"Good." Amos went inside. "Did they believe you?"

The young man followed him. "No."

"But you do."

"Yes."

Amos felt a softening toward this young man. He sat on his pallet and waited for the visitor to speak.

"Why do you live in such a mean place?"

"I would rather live in a cave, than trapped in the city."

The young man sat tensely. "I came back to explain why we're here and not in Jerusalem."

"Confess your reasons to God."

"God knows, and I want you to understand. There was not land or work enough for everyone in Jerusalem when my grandfather returned. I mean no disrespect, but the families who had lived and served in that district were not willing to step back and make room for others to serve."

Amos thought of Heled and Joram. The young man's words held the ring of truth. Like sheep, even the Levites had their butting order, and those long established in Jerusalem might have looked upon the influx of Levites with jaundiced eyes. He could not imagine Heled or others like him willingly giving up any of the benefits of their position, even to a brother in need.

"And I will confess—" the young man bowed his head—"Bethel has always been my home." He met Amos's eyes again. "My ancestors were born here."

"So you believe you belong here?"

"Perhaps God has kept me here for a reason."

"Do you follow after their ways?"

"Neither my father nor I nor any member of our family has bowed down to the golden calf, nor used the temple prostitutes."

"But you live comfortably in hypocrisy."

The young man's face reddened. "Would you have us live as they do?"

"Do they know you don't?"

"My father and I grieve over what you said about Judah."

"Grieving isn't enough to change God's mind." He leaned forward. "When our ancestors rebelled against the Lord in the desert, God was ready to wipe them out and make a dynasty of Moses' family. Moses pleaded for our salvation, and God changed His mind, withholding His wrath."

"Then you must pray for Judah!"

Amos nodded. "I have prayed, and will continue to do so, but I am *not* Moses."

"How many prayers will it take? My grandfather and father have prayed for years. I have prayed since I was a boy for Israel to return to God and for the tribes to reunite." The young man's eyes filled with tears. "Why is Jerusalem to be judged when Samaria and Bethel and Beersheba wallow in sin? You live here. You must see it even more clearly than I do. But it's different in Judea. King Uzziah worships the Lord our God and follows the Law. And Judah is to be consumed by fire?"

Lord, he speaks as I did. What is it in us that rejoices at the judgment upon others, while pleading that our sins be overlooked? "You will not be satisfied until everyone is dead. Better judgment should fall here on Israel than Judah. Is that it?"

"No. I did not mean that. I don't want that anyone should die."

"Then you are a better man than I. When the Lord first

gave me these visions, I felt the same exhilaration I see in these people. *Destroy Assyria! Yes, Lord.* I see the gloating faces, hear the cruel laughter. *Send fire on the fortresses of Philistia and Phoenicia. Yes, yes! Consume Edom with fire. Crush the Ammonites. Wipe out the Moabites!* He gave a mirthless laugh. "But Judah? *My* home? *My* family? We're better than the rest, aren't we?" He shook his head. "We haven't the excuse of ignorance. We know when we turn our backs on God. We make the choice to go our own way. Isn't that worse than what others do? They don't even know better."

"But Jerusalem. The Temple. God resides there!"

Amos shook his head. "No temple is large enough to contain the Lord our God."

"Perhaps I have seen more of Jerusalem and the Temple Mount than you have. Sin may not be as rampant there yet as it is here, but the Temple of the Lord stands there— if there is any place on earth that should stand firm upon the Law, shouldn't it be there?"

Amos sighed, weary, heartsick. A year ago, he wouldn't have cared about what happened to these people. And then he had prayed and God had answered. Now he cared so much that his heart broke every time he thought of Jerusalem, every time he entered the gates of Bethel, every time he looked into the faces of the people who could not stand before the judgment of a righteous God, least of all he. God was holding the nations accountable for what they'd done against His people, but the Lord would also hold His people accountable for the way they live before the nations. God chose them to be His people. He called them out of Egypt to be unique, an example to all the nations. And look how they lived, chasing after worthless idols. Thankless, faithless children. Lost sheep.

"Today, in Bethel, men heard the Word of the Lord against Judah and were silent. Judgment hit close to home this time again, but do they even wonder?"

The young man paled. "Wonder what?"

"If it applies to them. The Lord sees what men do. He hears what they say and how they live. The Lord knows we are like sheep, prone to wander. We cast ourselves into sin and can't get out. We look for better pastures among the religions of the nations around us and feed on poison. We drink from other men's wells and are infected with parasites. And still, the Lord sends prophets to call the people back to Him. But do they listen?"

"I'm listening."

"Yes." Amos's muscles relaxed. Why would God send him to Bethel if there was no hope?

"King David said God is faithful. His faithful love endures forever."

Amos had never given much thought to the word the shepherd-king had used. "His love *endures*."

God put up with their rebellious nature, suffered their rejection, and witnessed their desertion. God grieves over their lack of love. He sent prophet after prophet to call them back to Himself *before* He had to use His rod and staff of discipline. Even then, when discipline had to come, the Lord extended His mighty hand to deliver them again.

But then the cycle would repeat: faith for a generation, then complacency, soon followed by adultery as the people chased after false gods. Man decided how and what he wanted to worship and substituted idols for the living

God. Sin took root and spread tendrils of arrogance and pride into every area of life. Eyes became blind to God's presence, ears deaf to His Word. And the curses came again, often not even recognized for what they were— a call to return to the Lord.

"His faithful love endures forever."

There were far worse things than discipline. *A father who does not discipline his son hates him.* The same held true of a nation.

If the northern tribes refused to listen again, God would let them go their own way. They would continue to follow after Jeroboam, the son of Nebat.

"WHAT are you doing here?" Ahiam glared. "Get away from our stalls! Go back to Israel."

Amos stood shocked at his brother's greeting. "I've just come from offering my sacrifices to the Lord."

"Offer them in Bethel, you betrayer."

Heat surged into Amos's face. "I betray no one!"

When his brother took a swing at him, Amos blocked it with his staff, resulting in Ahiam's yelp of pain as he hit the ground. He scrambled up, ready to attack Amos again, but Bani put himself between them.

"People have heard what you've been saying in Bethel, Brother. They are not happy."

"Don't call him 'brother'!" Ahiam raged. "He makes nothing but trouble for us. He always has!"

"What trouble have I made?" Amos ground out and then sneered. "Is business down?"

"You! A prophet!" Ahiam laughed derisively. "You look like a beggar in your shepherd's rags."

"Better a poor man than a dishonest one."

With a roar, Ahiam came at him again. Amos hooked his shepherd's staff around Ahiam's leg and flipped him onto his back. Bani tried to intercede, but Amos shoved him back. "I told you both before I left that the Lord had given me visions of the nations." When Ahiam tried to rise, Amos held the end of the staff over him. "You wouldn't even listen to me!"

Ahiam slapped the shepherd's staff away and rose, face flushed.

Amos stepped forward. "God sent me to Bethel, Ahiam, and the prophecies are not mine, but the Lord's."

"You speak against Judah!" Ahiam spat on the ground. "That's what I think of you."

Amos went cold and then hot. "It is not me you spit upon, Brother."

"Enough!" Bani shouted at them.

Startled, the sheep leapt and moved restlessly in the stalls. Amos went over and spoke softly to the animals. Ahiam raised his hands in frustration.

Bani turned to Amos. "Tell us what's happened."

"I tried to tell you. When God called me to prophesy, I resisted." He looked between them. "You needn't tell me I'm unworthy. I know better than you both that I am not a learned man. What I know of God, I learned in the pastures and from the stars. God forgive me, I still resist Him." His mouth worked. "But I *must* speak what the Lord tells me."

Ahiam brushed himself off. "And we're supposed to believe He speaks destruction upon *us*?" He pointed north. "We, who are more faithful than that nation you now call your own?"

"I am Judean."

"Then *why*?"

"Because God wants it so. The northern tribes are still our brothers, though they wander like lost sheep with wolves for shepherds. We were once one flock! *Twelve* sons of Jacob, *twelve* tribes that God made into a nation. Have we all forgotten that?"

"Jeroboam claimed God gave him the ten northern tribes, and look what that usurper did with them!"

"And God sends me to remind them they yet belong to

the Lord. Why else would He send me to prophesy other than to confront their sin and call them back to Him?"

"It's not *their* sin you've confronted, is it? You cry down destruction on *us!* I'll bet they loved that message. I'll bet they paid you well."

Amos shook his head. "Who are we to be so self-righteous? We all sin against the Lord. Our family's wealth has grown out of it. And it will all turn to dust in our mouths if we don't repent."

"Don't preach at me." Ahiam flipped his hand, dismissing Amos's words. "We've known you since you were a baby messing yourself."

"A prophet is never heard in his own home or by his own family."

"You're misguided. You've been too long in the sun. You're beginning to bleat like your sheep."

"Careful what you say, Brother."

Something in Amos's voice silenced his brothers.

Bani spread his hands. "Forgive us if we have misunderstood. Tell us of the visions, Amos. Tell us everything."

"Yes." Ahiam's mouth twisted sardonically. "Tell us everything that we might be as wise as you."

Ignoring his older brother's sarcasm, Amos told them everything except the final vision he had yet to speak in Bethel.

Ahiam snorted. "Words to feed their pride. That's what you're giving them."

Sorrow filled Amos. "Pride goes before destruction, and haughtiness before a fall." He looked up at the Temple, then to the stalls of animals gained by deceit. He turned his gaze from the priests collecting fines to Bani and then to Ahiam. Grief overtook him, and fear for those he loved and could not convince. "Nothing is done in secret. The Lord sees what you do. He hears the words of your mouth. He knows what you hold most dear."

Ahiam frowned, but said nothing. Amos felt a moment of hope when he saw fear flicker in his brothers' eyes.

Fear of the Lord is the foundation of wisdom.

✦   ✦   ✦

"Make your offerings quickly," Bani said. "And give them to Elkanan or Benaniah. If Heled sees you, he will try to bar you from the Temple."

"Has he caused you trouble?"

"He is the one who told us of your prophecies against Judah."

"Is he unwilling to confess his sins before the Lord and repent?"

"It is no laughing matter, Amos!"

"Do you see me laughing?" He grasped Bani's arm. "Take the Lord's word to heart, Brother, before time runs out. I spoke the truth. Judah is judged! Repentance may bring mercy for a time, but you know as well as I how quickly men return to sin to make their own way in the world." Ahiam had given himself over to profits.

"And what would I do?"

"Be a shepherd again."

"Mishala would not be happy as a shepherd's wife, Amos."

"She would prefer it to being a widow. Without you, how will she live? How will she provide food for your children?" Many widows were forced to turn to prostitution for food money.

Amos gave his offerings and worshiped before the Lord. He spent the entire day inside the Temple, watching and listening. Not all the priests were like Heled, but the few who were had done great damage to the many who came with sincere hearts to worship the Lord.

I must keep my mind and heart fixed upon You, Lord, and not upon those who would lead me astray. How long had he allowed bitterness against Heled to rule his thinking?

He spent the night at his home in Tekoa. Eliakim gave him good reports about Ithai and Elkanan. They had faithfully obeyed Amos's instructions, and they had not traded spring lambs with Joram.

Amos walked with Eliakim to the boundary of his family's ancestral land. "If God allowed, I would stay."

Eliakim turned to him. "Will you return soon?"

"I will return to Jerusalem as often as the Law requires."

"I meant come home to stay. Here, in Tekoa."

"I know what you meant, Eliakim, but I don't know. I can only hope—" his throat tightened—"one day, perhaps, my friend. Look after everything as though I were here with you."

Eliakim bowed low. "May the Lord protect you."

"The eyes of the Lord are upon all the people, Eliakim. All His people." Judah and Israel might be God's chosen people, but the Lord rules the nations as well. Empires rise and fall at His command. Amos put his hand on Eliakim's shoulder. "God will strongly support the one whose heart is completely His." He looked back toward Jerusalem and thought of Bani and Ahiam. "Terrible days are coming."

He walked away, shoulders slumped with the burden

of the message he carried to Israel, the same message only
a few in Judah had heeded.

✦   ✦   ✦

The waiting was over.

Amos knew it the moment he entered the gates of
Bethel. The Spirit of the Lord came upon him, and he saw
everything differently. The beautiful woven veil of wealth
had been lifted to reveal the corruption and foulness hidden beneath. Everywhere he looked, he saw sin.

His anger mingled with sorrow. He saw his own sin,
too—his pride, his aloofness. He had withheld his love.
Now, he walked among the people of Israel as he had his
sheep, seeing both vulnerable lambs and dangerous predators.

The wealthy fed off the poor, stripping them of robes
and sandals as collateral for loans that could never be
repaid, while their wives lounged on Egyptian pillows in
their second-story summer houses decorated with inlaid
ivory furniture. Men hired to build in the city were cast
out, their wages withheld by the wealthy to buy drink
and delicacies.

The few men who dedicated themselves to the Lord as
Nazirites were persecuted. Ordered to show their fealty to
King Jeroboam, they drank wine before the elders who
knowingly forced them to break their vows to God.

Everyone ran to do evil on that mountain with its
golden calf. Incense smoke curled up from roofs. Mediums
who claimed they could interpret dreams sat before the
temple, grabbing their share of the offerings brought to
the royal sanctuary. Idol makers thrived. These people

were passionate for divination, and poured themselves out to wanton living and idol worship.

And yet God loved these lost people of Israel the way Amos loved and cared for his sheep. The truth shamed him and warmed his heart at the same time. And just as Amos sometimes found it necessary to wound a straying sheep in order to save it, so God must now discipline His straying people. If only they would listen, hear, before it was too late.

With new resolve, Amos strode up the street toward the temple of Bethel. "Come! Listen to the message that the Lord has spoken!"

"The prophet!"

"The prophet has returned!"

"Speak to us, Prophet!"

"Bring on the Day of the Lord!"

"We have been waiting for it to happen!"

"The nations will bow down before *us*!"

The excitement grew as Amos mounted the temple steps. He stopped halfway up and faced the people who stood eager to hear his words, certain he would proclaim continued prosperity and blessing. They nudged one another, gleeful, proud, stuffed with self-assurance. The square filled with excited people, all come to hear how God's wrath would be poured out on others. It was sin God hated, and here before him were a thousand sinners who believed they stood on firm foundations. They knew nothing.

Feed My sheep. . . .

Amos raised his staff. "This is what the Lord says: 'The people of Israel have sinned again and again, and I will not let them go unpunished!'"

"What is he saying about Israel?"

People murmured. People shifted. Some drew back slightly and began talking among themselves.

Amos pointed toward the priests gathered at the entrance of the temple. "They sell honorable people for silver and poor people for a pair of sandals. They trample helpless people in the dust and shove the oppressed out of the way."

A rumble began as people talked—confused, disappointed, angry.

Amos pointed toward the side streets and the temple brothels. "Both father and son sleep with the same woman, corrupting My holy name. At their religious festivals, they lounge in clothing their debtors put up as security. In the house of their god, they drink wine bought with unjust fines."

Faces flushed. Eyes narrowed. Mouths curled.

Amos threw his arms wide and cried out, "But as My people watched, I destroyed the Amorites, though they were as tall as cedars and as strong as oaks. I destroyed the fruit on their branches and dug out their roots. It was I who rescued you from Egypt and led you through the desert for forty years, so you could possess the land of the Amorites. I chose some of your sons to be prophets and others to be Nazirites."

Amos looked into dark, pitiless eyes. "'Can you deny this, My people of Israel?' asks the Lord."

He pointed to one, then another, and another. Faces hardening, they stared back.

He raised his staff again. "So I will make you groan like a wagon loaded down with sheaves of grain." Amos continued pointing as he came down the steps. "'Your fastest runners will not get away. The strongest among you will become weak. Even mighty warriors will be unable to save themselves. The archers will not stand their ground. The swiftest runners won't be fast enough to escape. Even those riding horses won't be able to save themselves. On that day the most courageous of your fighting men will drop their weapons and run for their lives!' says the Lord."

People cried out from every side, some in fear, others in rage.

"Lies! He speaks lies."

"There must be some mistake!"

"He's demon-possessed!"

"We are the chosen people! Look at how God has blessed us!"

"He's mad!"

They had cheered and celebrated judgment on other nations for brutality, slave trade, broken treaties, and desecration of the dead, but cried out in anger when confronted with their own sins.

How many months had he sat here on these steps and seen what they deemed sacred? An unholy mix of perversion and greed! They bowed down to their fleshly desires and exploited the poor without a twinge of conscience. They mocked the righteous, continuing to follow the Law while revering a band of robber priests who fleeced them of their money and, in return, gave back false hopes and promises of safety from a hollow idol that couldn't even protect itself.

"Listen to this message that the Lord has spoken. . . ."

"You prophesied against the nations. How can you now prophesy against us?"

"We have given you gifts and treated you kindly!"

"We believed you!"

"Listen to this message that the Lord has spoken. . . . " Amos cried out again.

"This is the thanks we get for taking care of a foreigner!"

"But the Lord sent him!"

"He *says* the Lord sent him. I'm not so sure."

Amos raised his hands. "Listen to this message that the Lord has spoken against you, O people of Israel and Judah: 'From among all the families on the earth, I have been intimate with you alone. That is why I must punish you for all your sins.'"

"No!" men shouted.

"Not us!" women wailed.

Children cried in confusion.

Temple guards surrounded Amos. "Come with us!"

When he tried to get through them, his staff was wrestled from him and he was taken by force.

"This way, Prophet." They hauled him up the steps and inside the temple.

"Let go of me!"

"Do you think you can start a riot on the temple steps and not answer for it?" The captain ordered him taken to Amaziah, the high priest. The guards hit and punched Amos until he sagged, then half dragged him through a shadowed corridor to a chamber. "Keep him here." The captain entered a room and spoke in hushed tones to several priests.

Amos wiped blood from his mouth.

After what seemed hours, a plainly gowned priest came out. "I am Paarai ben Zelek, son and servant of the most

high priest, Amaziah. You will come in now. Do not speak
unless you are spoken to, Prophet. Do you understand?"

Amos's heart raged within him. But the Lord held his
tongue.

Several priests stood talking to the high priest, who
gazed out a window that overlooked the square. He took
a long drink from a goblet, handed it to a servant, said
something under his breath to the others, and turned. His
head lifted as he studied Amos coldly. "I am Amaziah,
high priest of the temple of Bethel."

"And I am Amos, servant of the Lord our God."

Amaziah gestured for Amos to come forward. Amos
stood still, his gaze unfaltering.

The priest's eyes darkened. "We thought it best to
bring you here. For your own protection, of course."

"If you wish to protect the people, you will let them listen to the message that the Lord has spoken!"

A muscle tensed in Amaziah's cheek, but he spoke
calmly, even pleasantly. "You have thrilled our hearts
with your prophecies over the past eighteen months." His
eyes narrowed. "Why do you change your message now?"

"The message is not changed. Judgment is coming upon
the nations, Judah and Israel included. Unless we humble
our hearts and turn to the Lord, we have no hope."

The high priest spread his hands, the rich fabric of his
robes flowing like dark wings around him. "This is the
holy city." He raised his hands. "And this is the holy temple. You have lived here long enough to know our people
are devoted to God—more devoted to God than anyone in
Judah."

Amos went hot with fury. "Does that golden calf you
worship have ears that can hear your prayers? Does it feel

anything? Can it walk on its golden legs? Or utter one word from its golden throat?"

"Silence him!" Paarai commanded.

A guard hit him hard across the face.

Amaziah smiled faintly, eyes like obsidian. "You must not blaspheme the Lord."

"It is *you* who blaspheme the Lord."

The guards pummeled him until he lay half conscious on the floor. One kicked him hard in the side.

"Enough," Amaziah said and waved them away. "Lift him up."

A guard grabbed Amos and hauled him to his feet. Gritting his teeth, he kept from groaning aloud.

Amaziah reached for a golden pitcher. "A goblet of wine, perhaps. It is the finest in all Israel." When Amos didn't answer, he raised his brows. "No? A pity." He set the urn down. Crossing his arms, he tucked his hands into the heavy sleeves of his elaborately embroidered robe. "Why have you come to Bethel?"

"The Lord sent me to speak His Word to the people."

"And they have listened to you in growing numbers since you first entered our gates eighteen months ago. They have listened to your prophecies and brought offerings because of them."

Heat flooded Amos at the thought of those offerings being given to that hollow calf.

"The people have loved you." Amaziah smiled as he gently mocked. "Until today. Today, you spoke most unwisely, Amos."

"I spoke the truth."

"Truth as you see it, perhaps."

"I speak the words God gives me."

"Leave me alone with him."

"My lord?" The others protested.

Amaziah smiled and waved them away. "Paarai will remain with me."

Amos wondered what subterfuge the high priest intended to try. *Lord, give me wisdom*. The attending priests entered a side room, and the guards remained outside the door.

"You are not the only man to see visions, my young friend. I have had many visions over my years in the priesthood and received abundance because of them. And I tell you God's blessing is upon Israel. It is evident for all who have eyes to see. Look around you! We have wealth. We live in a time of great prosperity. We serve King Jeroboam, and he is as great as his grandfather, who was greater than Solomon's son Rehoboam."

Amaziah shook his head. "And yet you would tell our people we face destruction? We are strong enough now that no enemy dares come against us." He clicked his tongue. "You should go back to your sheep. The people will not listen to you now. You have overstayed your welcome." He shook his head in condescension. "We have nothing to fear from you."

"From me, no. But you should fear the Lord."

"Fear the one we love? Even after all these months of sitting on the temple mount and wandering our streets, you have learned so little about our people. You are blind and deaf. Have you missed the crowds who flock to the temple to give offerings to our god? Have you been deaf to their songs of praise? Have you failed to see the wealth of the temple itself? Our people are far more devout in worship and happy in life than those in Judah."

"I see those who prey on the poor, your rich women who eat like cows. They fatten themselves for the slaughter!"

"Father, do not allow him to speak—"

"Be quiet!" Amaziah's lips whitened. He spoke to his son as he glared at Amos. "A few stubborn fools still return to Jerusalem to worship, but they will not go back to the old ways. Nor do they need to. They have all they want right here."

Amos glared back. "Not for long." *Let these wicked 'priests' be disgraced, Lord. Silence their lying lips. Don't let them live long lives of leisure.*

Amaziah smiled coldly. "If you have such a calling to become a priest, why don't you bring us what is required and become one? We would welcome you to our society." He looked at Paarai. "Wouldn't we?"

Paarai hesitated and then agreed.

Amos narrowed his eyes. "Only a Levite can be a priest of the Lord."

"But apparently anyone can be a prophet." Amaziah smirked as he took in Amos's old clothes, his sandaled feet. "Here, in Bethel, you can be a priest *and* a prophet. That is the way it's done."

Paarai smiled.

Amos looked between them. "Once, we were one nation under God."

"You live in the past, Amos. It is unwise."

"Are you threatening to kill me?"

"If I wanted to see you dead, I would have left you to the mob." Amaziah clucked his tongue. "You disappointed them today."

"I told them the truth."

The high priest's eyes flashed. "Where is your evidence? Where is the lightning and thunder? Nor have your other prophecies proven true. Had even one come about, your name would be great in Israel, and your place among the prophets assured. But all is as it has been. Nothing has changed. We merely grow stronger while you crow like a rooster."

Paarai chuckled. "Careful you do not cause so much disruption you end up in a stew."

Amos saw them clearly. Evil men who had no fear of God to restrain them. In their blind conceit, they couldn't see how vile they really were. Everything they had said thus far was crooked and deceitful. "Everything will happen just as the Lord has said, and it will happen in His time, not yours."

"We await the Day of the Lord as eagerly as you do." Amaziah's voice took on lofty tones. "For in that day, all our enemies will be put under our heel!"

"So speaks the Lord." Paarai's eyes glowed.

The Spirit of the Lord took hold of Amos and spoke through him. "What sorrow awaits you who say, 'If only the Day of the Lord were here!' You have no idea what you are wishing for. That day will bring darkness, not light."

Amaziah's eyes went black. "You do not listen well, do you? Some men must learn the hard way." He raised his voice. "Guards, take him! Give him twenty lashes and send him on his way." He pointed at Amos. "Your false prophecies will gain you nothing. The people will never listen to you!"

"Repent! For judgment is at hand."

Paarai smirked as the guards entered and took hold of Amos. "Get him out of here."

+ + +

It was night when Amos was thrown out of the temple. He fell down the steps, banging his shins, his shoulder, his head. As he lay at the bottom, he heard a voice from above him.

"Don't forget this!"

His staff clattered down the steps. He reached for it, using it to brace himself as he slowly stood. On fire with pain, shoulder and head aching, Amos managed to stumble from the square.

"There he is. . . ."

Fearful of another beating, Amos hurried down a narrow street. A wave of dizziness came over him and he fell against a wall. He clutched his staff, his only defense. But someone grasped it and held it still.

"Let me help you, Amos." The voice was familiar. Amos looked up. Though his vision was blurred, he recognized the young Levite who had come to ask him questions about Judah.

"You . . ."

"This is the man I've told you about, Father." He slipped his arm around Amos. "When the guards took you inside the temple, I went for my father. We've been waiting. . . ."

Amos groaned in pain.

The older man took charge. "We will take him home with us and see to his wounds."

The two men lifted him to his feet and supported him on each side. "Easy."

"Our house is not far from here, Amos."

They half carried him down a street, around a corner, and through a doorway. Amos lifted his head enough to see the dimly lit room. A woman asked whom they had brought.

"The man I told you about, Mother. The prophet of the Lord our God."

"Oh! What have they done to him?"

"We'll explain later, Jerusha." The father sent her for water as they helped Amos to a pallet.

Amos fought the waves of nausea.

"Rest, now. You are safe here." The older man squeezed his shoulder. "You are fortunate your skull didn't crack like a melon on those steps."

"I have a hard head."

The elder man smiled grimly. "A prophet of the Lord needs one. I am Beeri. Jerusha is my wife."

She knelt and began to gently wash his bruised and bleeding face. "Our son, Hosea, has told us much about you."

Amos took the damp cloth from Jerusha's hand. "I will see to my own wounds."

She blushed. "I did not wish to offend. . . . "

"You didn't. I must go. I do not want to bring trouble on you." When he tried to get up, he gasped in pain.

All three protested. "There is nowhere for you to go, Amos. The gates are closed for the night. You can't sleep out in the cold. Stay with us. Please!"

Amos sank back with a grimace.

Hosea hunkered down before him. "His eyes are swelling shut, Father."

"We have balm that will help heal his wounds."

Jerusha crossed the room and took something from a cupboard.

Darkness closed in, and Amos felt gentle hands lower him.

When next he opened his eyes, moonlight streamed through a high window. He saw Hosea sleeping on a nearby pallet. A small clay lamp cast a soft glow, by which he could see a table, two small benches, some storage urns, bowls, a water jug, a cabinet built into the wall. Every bone and muscle in his body ached when he pushed himself up.

Hosea also sat up. "You're awake!"

"Barely."

"How do you feel?"

"As though someone whipped me and threw me down some stone steps."

"You've lain like death for three days."

So long! He remembered none of it. "May the Lord bless you for your kindness." Had he made it outside the city, he might have been lying in a field somewhere, unconscious and prey to scavengers.

"How is your head?"

Amos felt the bandages. He had a slight headache, but the dizziness was gone. "I'll live." His stomach growled loudly.

"It will be morning soon." Hosea grinned. "My mother will make bread."

Amos smiled.

"It is good to have you as our guest, Amos." He grimaced. "Despite the circumstances, of course."

Amos rubbed his head. A bump still protruded, but it was not as tender as the day he had received it. He still had trouble seeing, and realized after a slight exploration that his eyelids were swollen almost shut.

"I can't serve you bread, but there is some wine."

"A little wine and I'd probably sleep for another two days. Water, please." Amos found his staff beside the pallet and struggled to rise.

Hosea helped him. "Please. Don't go. Everyone shouted so loudly in the square I could not hear what you had to say. I want to know what you prophesied about Israel."

"It is the Lord's Word and not mine that stands against Israel for all its many sins."

"You said God will punish Damascus, Gaza, Tyre, Edom, Ammon, Moab, and Judah. And now God will bring judgment on Israel as well. The entire world is condemned. Not one nation will remain standing after God's judgment."

Amos sank wearily onto the bench and leaned his forearms on the table. "Judah will be the last to fall."

"Is there hope if Judah repents?"

"There is always hope when a nation repents." But they seldom did. It took famine, drought, or flood to bring a nation to its knees before God. It took war!

Hosea poured water and handed the cup to Amos. "But Judah will still fall in the end?"

Amos drank deeply and held out the cup for more. "Men fell long ago and still refuse the hand of God to help them rise again." He drained the cup again.

"What then will be left, Amos?"

"God's promise, my young friend. You reminded me that His faithful love endures forever. So it does. His mercy is poured out upon those who love Him. The eyes of the Lord search the whole earth in order to strengthen those whose hearts are fully committed to Him. Destruction will come as surely as the sun rises in the morning, but a remnant will remain. Men like you who love the Lord and want to follow Him. The rest will be like chaff in the wind, here one day and gone the next."

"I should feel more hope than I do. I feel I must do something to help you."

"*Listen*. And encourage others to do likewise. And then do what the Lord commands."

The sun rose and with it Beeri and Jerusha. She prepared the morning meal. They prayed and broke bread together.

"Why don't you stay here in Bethel, Amos?" Hosea looked at his father. "Wouldn't it be far better for him to live here with us?"

Beeri nodded.

Amos fought the temptation. "More convenient, perhaps, but dangerous for you. I have a place to live."

"At least stay a few more days." Jerusha offered him more bread. "Until you've recovered from your fall."

Amos thanked them.

After another day, Amos longed to stay. He enjoyed the conversations with Beeri and Hosea that lasted far into the night, always centering on the Lord and His commandments.

Beeri worked as a scribe, and Hosea studied the scrolls his father kept in the cabinet. Jerusha used what little money they had wisely. Beeri read from the Scriptures locked in the cabinet each evening. Much he knew by memory, and Hosea along with him. "They were taken away once," Beeri told him, "but I had another copy hidden."

Beeri questioned Amos only once. "How is it a prophet of God does not know the Scriptures?"

"I've spent my life in the pastureland with my sheep. Other than a few years when I was a boy, I've had little opportunity to sit before a rabbi and learn the Law. What I know is given to me by God."

Beeri was quick to apologize. "I did not mean to question your calling, Amos."

"I take no offense, but I will say that had I had the opportunity, I doubt I could do as you have done. Some men have minds that can take in knowledge, like you and Hosea. What I know is the land, the night skies, my sheep."

Beeri nodded. "That is a great deal in itself, my friend."

"The Lord is our shepherd," Hosea said. "Surely the Lord sent you here to show us the way home."

"I've usually had to deal with a few wayward sheep." Amos shook his head. "But never an entire flock such as Israel so determined to find trouble."

After six days Amos knew he must leave. Here, in this quiet, devout household, he slept comfortably, ate well, and enjoyed warm fellowship. But, in this small dwelling tucked away in the labyrinth of Bethel, among these hospitable people, he could not hear the Lord's voice as he could when he stood beneath the stars in an open field.

"I must go."

"Back to Jerusalem?" Hosea leaned forward, eager. "Say the word and I will go with you!"

"No. I must go out into the hills and return to my place of rest."

"But it's only a cave."

"I've slept at the entrance of many caves, Hosea. It is a

sheepfold and reminds me of the simpler life I had before the Lord called me to come to Bethel."

Jerusha looked downcast, Beeri confused. "Surely this is more comfortable than a cave."

"Yes, it is." But distracted by the pleasure of their company, he could not clear his mind long enough to hear the quiet Voice that directed his footsteps and his words.

Neither Hosea nor his father tried to convince him otherwise. Jerusha filled his scrip with roasted grain and raisins, almonds and barley bread.

Just before dusk, Hosea walked with him to the city gate. When he started to follow Amos outside, Amos turned.

"Go back, Hosea. Convince your father to move to Judah. Go to Tekoa and speak with my servant, Eliakim. Tell him I sent you. He will help you find a priest in Jerusalem to help you get settled. I know it will be difficult to start over there, but you have no future here."

Hosea nodded. "I will tell my father everything you have said."

"May the Lord bless you and protect you. May the Lord smile on you and be gracious to you. . . ." He could not finish.

Hosea clasped his hand. "May the Lord show you His favor and give you His peace."

Amos walked away, shoulders bent and aching. *Spare them, Lord. Pluck them out of the destruction to come. Especially young Hosea, who has such a hunger and thirst for You.*

✦   ✦   ✦

The first night proved the most difficult, for after days with kind friends, loneliness set in and with it a longing to go home to Tekoa and his sheep. The Lord spoke to him in his dreams. When Amos awakened with the dawn, he rose with renewed strength.

Return to Bethel and speak to My people again.

He knew what he must do. If it meant another lashing, another beating, or even death, Amos would do what the Lord called him to do.

Still bruised and sore, he limped down the hill and stood at the gates, waiting for them to open. When they did, he went forward, staff in hand.

The guard looked far from pleased. "You!"

Without a word, Amos walked past him and up the street. He stood in the temple square. "The idols you've made will disgrace you. They are frauds. They can do nothing for you. The Lord your God is the Creator of everything that exists, and you are His special possession. Come back to Him. Turn away from godless living and sinful pleasures. We should live in this world with self-control, right conduct, and devotion to God!"

The few who paused to listen quickly changed their minds and passed him by. Guards stood at the temple doorway, sniggering.

After a week, the temple guards locked him in stocks.

✦   ✦   ✦

Issachar came in the night and spoke from behind a pillar. "You should say the things you first said, Amos. Then you wouldn't be locked up in the stocks. You wouldn't be a joke to everyone who passes by."

Amos lifted his head. Had Issachar come only to taunt? "I speak the Word of the Lord." Exhausted, every muscle aching, hungry, thirsty, he fought the depression filling him. "You would do well to heed it."

After a nervous glance around, Issachar came out and stood before him. "You've only to look around Bethel to see how God has blessed us!" He spoke low, half pleading, half frustrated.

Amos felt Issachar's tension. He watched him look around and edge back toward the deeper shadows. "Fear God, not men."

Issachar leaned close, angry. "I'm here for your own good. Stop speaking against Israel. You insult us!"

"God gives you an opportunity to repent."

"*Raca!* Fool. You're going to get yourself killed if you keep on this way." He disappeared into the night without offering so much as a piece of dried bread or a sip of water.

"This is your hour, Issachar. The hour of darkness." Amos wept softly.

✦   ✦   ✦

Though he became a joke in Bethel, he did not stop speaking the Word of the Lord after he was released from the stocks.

Every morning, he came into city. Every day, he spoke.

No one listened. No one left gifts at the entrance of his cave anymore. His only regret over that was not having anything to offer the poor he saw each time he entered the city, the men whose robes and sandals had been stripped from them as collateral for debts they would never be able to pay. Amos writhed inwardly over the mercilessness of the rich. He could only offer encouragement to the poor whose outer garments had not been returned when the night chill set in. "The Lord hears your prayers." Even they would not listen to him.

He saw the widow in the marketplace again. She saw him as well and turned her back to him, ordering her hungry children to do the same.

No one listened to him anymore. Those who had so relished the first prophecies turned deaf ears to anything said against Israel.

Lord, when they see me on the street, they turn the other way. I am ignored as if I were dead!

For six months, he stood waiting at the gates in the morning and departed just before they were shut at night. Day after day, Amos preached the Word of the Lord and day after day, he suffered mockery and disdain. The neophyte priests gloated while Amaziah watched balefully from a high temple window.

Even as he cried out the truth, people walked up the steps and into the temple of Bethel, day by day sealing their fate with their indifference toward the Lord. Life and death were before them.

And they continued to embrace death with foolish abandon.

✦   ✦   ✦

"Listen to the message that the Lord has spoken!"

"He's back again," people muttered.

"Who is he?" visitors to the city asked.

"Just a self-proclaimed prophet. He never says anything good."

"He just harps on and on about our sins."

"Don't pay any attention. He's mad."

Someone bumped Amos. "Go back to your sheep!"

Another bumped, harder this time, almost knocking him from his feet. "We're not a bunch of sheep you can herd."

Another shoved him. No one made an effort to stop them.

Amos raised his staff. "Listen, O Israel. You have sinned against the Lord your God!"

The youths backed off, laughing and cursing him.

"Why don't you shut up!" someone shouted. "We spend more time worshiping the Lord than you do! All you do is talk and talk."

Others took up the cry. "He talks and talks."

Others laughed. "And nothing happens."

Amos looked at his tormentors. "Can two people walk together without agreeing on the direction? Does a lion ever roar in a thicket without first finding a victim? Does a young lion growl in its den without first catching its prey? Does a bird ever get caught in a trap that has no bait? Does a trap spring shut when there's nothing to catch? When the ram's horn blows a warning, shouldn't the people be alarmed?"

"And I suppose you're the trumpet?"

Men and women laughed. "Listen to him trumpet doom!"

Amos kept on. "Does disaster come to a city unless the Lord has planned it?"

"What disaster, Prophet? Where?"

"Just ignore him. He doesn't know what he's talking about."

People walked away.

Amos raised his voice. "Indeed, the Sovereign Lord

never does anything until He reveals His plans to His servants the prophets. The lion has roared—"

"Sounds more like a mewing kitten to me!"

More laughter.

"So who isn't frightened? The Sovereign Lord has spoken—so who can refuse to proclaim His message?"

"Go back to your cave in the hills!"

"No wonder he speaks of lions and birds. He lives like an animal."

Amos paced on the temple steps. "Announce this to the leaders of Philistia and to the great ones of Egypt: 'Take your seats now on the hills around Samaria, and witness the chaos and oppression in Israel.'"

"You said Philistia was to be destroyed! Have you changed your mind?"

"False prophet!"

"He makes no sense."

"'Therefore,' says the Sovereign Lord, 'an enemy is coming! He will surround them and shatter their defenses!'" Amos shouted, his throat raw from speaking. "Then he will plunder all their fortresses." Filled with the Spirit of the Lord, Amos strode up a few steps, standing below the entrance to the temple of Bethel. "This is what the Lord says: 'A shepherd who tries to rescue a sheep from a lion's mouth will recover only two legs or a piece of an ear.' So it will be when the Israelites in Samaria are rescued—" Amos's voice caught—"with only a broken bed and a tattered pillow."

Tears ran down his cheeks. "'Now listen to this, and announce it throughout all Israel,' says the Lord, the Lord God of Heaven's Armies. 'On the very day I punish Israel

for its sins, I will destroy the pagan altars at Bethel. The
horns of the altar will be cut off and fall to the ground.'"

The ground beneath Amos trembled.

"Did you feel that?" someone spoke in alarm.

Amos's lungs filled. Fire and strength poured through
his body. "And I will destroy the beautiful homes of the
wealthy—their winter mansions and their summer houses,
too—all their palaces filled with ivory—" Amos roared
like a lion—"*says the Lord!*"

Another tremor, longer this time.

People looked at one another. "What's happening?"

The ground rolled; the earth quaked.

Some cried out. Others screamed.

A low rumble sounded from the depths of the earth.
The giant stones of the temple grated against each other.
People poured outside, shrieking with terror. They covered their heads. A section of the portico fell with a
mighty crash, shattering stone in all directions. People fled
down the steps. Some tripped and fell, tumbling, taking
others down with them. A dozen disappeared beneath the
falling wall of a temple brothel. Broken lamps spread
ignited oil that fed on the expensive Babylonian draperies,
and smoke billowed from summer houses.

People knocked one another down in their panic. A
woman in her finery lay trampled at the base of the temple
steps.

Bumped and jostled by the fleeing crowd, Amos fought
to maintain his balance.

*Oh, God, don't let it be too late. Have mercy upon them!
Have mercy. . . .*

Amos saw a mother and child trampled on the street. By
the time he reached them, they were dead.

Surrounded by screams of terror, Amos braced himself and raised his staff. "Repent before it's too late!" Dust billowed around him. *"Repent!"*

The din of chaos and terror swallowed his voice.

FIVE

EVEN when the earthquake ended, dust continued to billow from collapsing buildings and portions of the city wall. The screaming subsided, and people moved around in shock, climbing over the debris-filled streets as they called for loved ones. Many were trapped inside buildings.

Every few hours, the earth trembled again, with less violence than before. But with each aftershock, the people's fear rose. Some panicked and fled the city, leaving the helpless to cry pitifully for help. Others worked frantically to uncover family members. Many died, crushed beneath their ashlar houses.

Amos stayed to help. "There's another over here!" He lifted stones carefully so that he wouldn't cause others to fall inward on the moaning person beneath the pile.

"Amos . . ." A soft groan came from beneath the rubble, a bloody hand extended.

Amos worked quickly, carefully, and uncovered Issachar.

"Amos . . ." He grasped Amos's hand tightly. His mouth moved, but no words came. His eyes pleaded as he coughed. Blood trickled from the corner of his mouth. His hand gripped tighter, eyes filled with fear. He choked.

Amos stayed with him until his struggle ended. Then he rose to help others. "Here! There's another here!"

People scrambled over fallen stones. Some came to help. Others used the confusion to steal whatever they could grab.

"Stop, thief! Stop him! He's stealing from my shop!"

A young man raced down the street, leaping over rub-

ble as a goldsmith cried for help. Amos ignored the thief as
he lifted another stone. A naked prostitute stared up at
him with dead eyes. The man who had shared her bed had
been crushed beneath a wall.

"Help me. . . ." A weak voice came from farther back,
inside the tumbled structure.

A hand protruded from a narrow hole, fingers moving
as though to seek the light. "Help me, please." A woman's
broken voice.

Amos took her hand. "I'm here." Her fingers tightened
as she sobbed. After removing several stones and fallen
timbers, he reached her. He grabbed a Babylonian drapery
to cover her. She cried out in pain as he lifted her and carried her over the rubble. Placing her gently on the stones
of the courtyard, he left her among other wounded.

A priest appeared at the top of the temple steps, his
vestments dust covered. He scrambled over the fallen
stones and made his way down the steps. When he
reached the bottom, he looked at Amos, face ashen with
shock. "Did you do this to us, Prophet?"

"Am I God that I can make the world tremble?"

"The horns of the altar are broken! And the golden
calf . . ."

Amos felt exultant. "What? You mean it couldn't run
away and save itself?"

"Blasphemy!"

"Look around you, Priest. Look and be warned! If you
set up that golden calf again, worse will befall the people.
You will be the goat that leads them to slaughter!"

Another aftershock rattled the doors of the temple, and
the priest's eyes went wide with fear. Dodging falling
stones, he stumbled away, joining another holy man who

had managed to run from the temple with the first wave of terrified worshipers, and now sat bereft and confused. Watching Amos, they leaned close and talked.

Amaziah came out of the temple. Clearly shaken, he stared at Amos.

"Come and help your people!" Amos shouted, but the old man ducked inside again.

Night began to fall. Dozens of people still needed help. Amos worked through the night, resting when he could not go on. When he could do no more, he made his way to the city gate that stood open, damaged.

Guards shouted orders. "Heave! Again! Heave!" Rock tumbled.

Bodies had been laid out in a line outside the walls, awaiting burial.

This is not the vision I saw, Lord. This was not devastation. This was only a sound shaking, a warning to listen.

He overheard two merchants. "Jerusalem is worse off than we are."

Jerusalem! Horrified, Amos ran down the road. Had Bani and Ahiam survived? What of their wives and children?

Stumbling, he stopped to pull the hem of his long robe up between his knees and tuck it securely into his belt. His fear had overtaken his reason. He couldn't run all the way to Jerusalem. Setting off again at a brisk walk, he tried to restrain his panic.

Nearly three hours later, he reached the top of a hill and leaned on his staff to catch his breath, seeing Jerusalem in the distance. Solomon's Temple caught the sunlight and shone brilliant white and gold. Amos gave a cry of relief.

Tents dotted the hillsides, sheltering the hundreds who

had left the city until the aftershocks subsided. Everywhere was the din of human voices as people searched for
friends and family members. Donkeys brayed. Camels bel-
lowed.

Merchants lined the road to Jerusalem with their
booths.

"Tents of the finest goatskin!"

"Water jars!"

"Oil lamps!"

"Blankets."

Supplies had been brought from other towns and were
being dispensed by soldiers keeping order.

The Sheep Gate stood open and still intact. Amos
pressed his way through the throng and headed toward
the Temple Mount. If he didn't find Bani and Ahiam near
their stalls, he would go to their homes.

He spotted his brothers repairing a pen while young
boys kept the nervous sheep contained. "Bani! Ahiam!"
He ran and embraced each of them. "You are alive!" He
drew back and looked them over. "You are not hurt?"

"You're shaking, little brother." Bani took Amos by the
arm and made him sit. Dipping a gourd cup into a barrel of
water, he held it out.

"I came as soon as I heard. . . ." Amos drank deeply.
"Bethel was struck also. The damage is horrendous." He
wiped droplets of water from his beard.

Ahiam looked up at the Temple. "God did this because
King Uzziah sinned."

Amos raised his head. "Sinned? How?"

"Three days ago, he went into the Temple with a censor
in his hand and lit the incense."

It was a great sin, indeed, to usurp the privileges

ordained by God to the priesthood. Had Uzziah attempted to take over the Temple and do things his own way just as Jeroboam, the son of Nebat, had done?

Bani handed Amos another cup of water. "The priests were in an uproar trying to stop him."

Ahiam pointed. "I was over there when the king came up the hill. I knew something was happening, so I followed the entourage inside. Several of the priests met the king and argued with him."

"I heard the uproar from here. It sounded like a riot. I went running to see what was going on."

"Even the high priest couldn't dissuade Uzziah," Ahiam said. "The king intended to make a fragrant offering to the Lord, and no one was going to stop him."

"The minute he lit—"

"Let *me* tell him!" Ahiam gave Bani a shove. "I was there, not you."

"So tell him!"

Amos grew impatient. "One of you tell me; it matters not which."

Ahiam waved his hand. "The moment King Uzziah lit the incense, he was covered with leprosy. I've never heard a man scream like that. The judgment of the Lord was on him and he knew it! The priests rushed him out of the Temple."

"And then the earthquake started."

"Only minor damage to the Temple," Ahiam said, "though I thought it would come down on our heads."

"Some areas of the city were hit hard. Hundreds are homeless."

"Your homes?"

"Both need repair, but at least we still have roofs over our heads. And our wives and children are safe."

"Where is King Uzziah now?"

"No one knows for sure. In seclusion. Somewhere outside the city, safe and guarded. His son, Jotham, brought guilt offerings yesterday and today."

"And the priests have been in constant prayer since it happened."

Ahiam straightened and went back to work fitting two rails together. "Our situation has changed over the past few days."

Somewhat rested, Amos stood and gave him a hand. "How do you mean?"

Bani answered. "Heled was killed. Squashed like a bug under a fallen building." He gave a short, mirthless laugh. "At a money changer's office."

Amos saw that fear of the Lord had taken root in Ahiam's eyes. For Amos, it was a spark of hope in a sea of darkness. *Let it grow, Lord. Let it flourish into awe and worship so that my brothers might not sin against You again.* "God sees what men do. He knows their hearts."

"So you have said. Perhaps you should tell me again what you saw. I failed to listen last time you were here."

Amos did tell him. All day, they talked. When he went to Bani's house, the family gathered. They listened, quiet and intent, grim-faced and with a fear that went deeper than what had been aroused by the earthquake.

Amos awakened in the predawn hours. The clay lamp cast a soft glow. Ahiam sat silent, staring at him.

Sitting up slowly, Amos looked back at him, and frowned. "What's wrong?"

"Stay here, Amos. Stay in Jerusalem. Speak to our people about what the Lord has told you."

Amos shook his head. God had already sent a prophet to Jerusalem. "Listen to Isaiah. I must go where God called me to go."

Ahiam lowered his eyes. "If all you say is true . . ."

"If?"

Ahiam lifted his head. "A prophet is seldom recognized by his own family, Amos. You know how I've doubted you." He grimaced. "Because you're my brother. My *younger* brother. I've known you since you were a baby. You've always been hotheaded and opinionated. And now you—" he struggled for words—"you speak with authority. I believe you, Amos, but God help my unbelief."

"Nothing I've said has not been said before by God Himself. He made it known to us from the beginning. We've simply forgotten." Amos shook his head. "No. Not forgotten. We *rejected* His Word. He told us of the blessings He would pour upon us if we followed Him. He also warned us of the cursings if we turned our backs on Him. It's all there in the Scriptures." Beeri had read them aloud to him. "Though the priests may speak little of it these days."

"Even where there was obedience, Amos, there was hardship."

"Of course. Life is hard. Knowing God makes a vast difference in how we live. Don't you long to see that cloud overhead again? that pillar of fire that kept the darkness back?" How Amos longed for those days when there was physical evidence of God's presence. But even then, men refused to believe. "When I have heard God's voice speak to me, I have felt *alive,* Ahiam. Even when I have not rejoiced at the message I must carry, I rejoice that He still speaks to men, even simple shepherds like me."

"If you asked God, would He listen to your prayer? Would He let you stay here among your brethren?"

"I did ask, Ahiam. I spent months out in the pasture-land arguing and pleading with the Lord to take this burden from me." He shook his head. "I must go back to Israel."

"But you've told them what will come! You've done what God sent you to do."

"They've yet to hear."

"You told them! If they refuse to listen, then their blood is on their own heads. I've heard about the way you were treated. They welcomed the judgments upon the nations around them. They even rejoiced when they heard Judah would be overrun by enemies. Has anything changed?"

Amos shrugged. He had been popular for a while. He had drawn crowds until he told them what the Lord said about Israel. The priests had always watched him with jaundiced eyes, coveting the crowds who gathered to hear him speak. As long as the prophecies focused on the sins of the surrounding nations, they could say little against him without the people wondering why. But as soon as the Lord focused His judgment upon Israel, all restraints were removed. It had been easy to drive the frightened, angry flock back into the stall of the golden calf and serve them up to idol worship.

"They didn't listen, did they?" Ahiam challenged. "Not any more than I did."

"No. They didn't. Perhaps the earthquake will open their eyes and ears as it has yours. Now is the time to speak. Now, before it's too late."

"For how long, Amos?"

"How long does it take to decide to turn back from destruction, Ahiam? One word from the Lord may be enough now to make them repent and trust in God again."

"One decision isn't enough, Amos. Don't you understand? They will hear you for a day, a week, maybe a month or two. But they must decide each day what they will do. Each and every day, from now on."

"What hope can they find in the protection of golden idols and pagan worship? It's all smoke, Ahiam, sweet-smelling and deadly."

"They may not find truth, Amos, but they find pleasure. God has allotted seventy years to men—maybe more, maybe less. That's not long on this earth. And you said yourself, life is difficult. They have shaken off the burden of the Law. They won't easily shoulder it again." He rose. "They will turn on you, Amos. They will tear you to pieces like a pack of wolves."

"Yes. Or they may repent."

"Israel, Judah. We share the same blood. I believe you now, Amos, and yet, I don't believe you. I want to believe God is the one who rules, but forty-five years in the shadow of the Temple has shown me how men work— men like Heled."

"Heled is dead. You're free."

"Free of him. Free to wonder who will try to enslave me now." Ahiam looked away, the muscle working in his jaw. "I can only hope to align myself with priests who fear the Lord." He turned back to Amos. "As you did, Brother. As you taught Ithai and Elkanan. But there are precious few you can trust these days."

"More today than yesterday!" The earthquake would shake men's souls.

"Perhaps." Ahiam gave him a tight smile. "Time will tell, won't it?"

Amos put on his outer robe. "I must go."

Ahiam grasped his arm. "Don't. Stay here." Tears filled his eyes. "Help us rebuild."

A surge of emotion swept through Amos. If he stayed, he would be disobeying God. The priests of Israel would not easily release their hold on the lost sheep they had rustled from God and now held captive with lies. Amos's eyes grew hot and moist, for he knew Ahiam did not understand the spiritual battle that raged in Amos. He missed his family. He loved Judah. But Amos felt the stirring within his soul. The call to go back to Bethel. If he didn't . . .

"The safest place I can be is in the will of God, Ahiam."

"They will kill you."

"I can't think about that. I must speak. I am compelled to do so. The Word burns in my soul like a consuming fire." God cared passionately about His people. God fathered and mothered mankind, and yet His children wandered away in the wilderness. "I must call out to them, Ahiam." God had sent him to call Israel home to Him, to warn them of punishment if they refused. For to keep going the way they were meant eternal death, separation from God for all time.

Amos took up his belt, wound it around his waist, and tied it securely. "Do not make me question what God calls me to do." He put on his sandals.

Ahiam followed him out the door. "You're my brother, Amos. We've had our differences, but . . . I love you."

An admission choked out and all the more precious.

Amos embraced him tightly. "Better if you love God." He took his staff and left.

+   +   +

A cry went up from the watchtower as Amos came up the road to Bethel. "The prophet! The prophet returns!"

He stopped when a dozen well-armed warriors poured out the gate. Heart in his throat, he clutched his staff. Did they intend to arrest him? Would they drag him into their temple this time, place him on trial, and execute him?

The warriors took their places in two perfect lines on either side of the road, backs rigid, eyes straight ahead. The elders waited before the gate. Amos drew air into his lungs, straightened, and walked forward. He stopped, face-to-face with the judges and elders. A crowd gathered on the wall and behind the open gates.

"You have returned to us."

He could not tell if they were pleased or dismayed, but the fear in their eyes was evident. "Yes. I have returned." These people burdened his heart and mind.

"Do you have more to tell us?"

"I will speak only what the Lord gives me to speak."

They all began talking at once. They praised and pleaded, cajoled and flattered. Foolishly, they thought a prophet held the power to bring about natural disasters.

He raised his hands. "Quiet! Listen to me. It is the Lord you should fear. Not I. I bring you His Word, but power rests in *His* hands!"

"But will you be our advocate?" One of the judges came forward. "Will you plead for us before God?"

He had not been called by God to be their advocate, but to warn them to repent, to tell them of what lay ahead if they did not. Though they slay him, he must speak the truth. Life and death lay before them; they must choose. "The eyes of the Lord watch over those who do right, and He hears their prayers."

"Will God leave us alone? Or does He intend to bring further disaster on us?"

Amos looked around at the faces pressed close and waiting for his answer. "The Lord has told you what He will do if you don't repent. He turns His face against those who do evil, and He will erase the memory of them from the earth."

A nervous twitter ran through the crowd. An elder spoke. "When you first came to us, all your prophecies were against our enemies. Why do you now turn against us? Why do you call down destruction upon a city devoted to worship?"

Angry, Amos stepped toward the accuser. "I have spoken openly for two years, and you have not heard a word of what I've said!" He thrust out his staff, pointing up the street. "If that golden calf you love had any power at all, would it have been toppled from its altar?" People moved back from him as he searched their faces. "The Sovereign Lord never does anything until He reveals His plans to His servants the prophets. I have told you the Word of the Lord. *If* you listen, *if* you learn, *if* you turn your hearts and minds fully to the Lord your God, perhaps He will change His mind and withhold judgment."

"Then teach us," someone called from the back. "I will listen."

"So will I!"

"As will I!"

So many spoke in quick agreement. Was their acquies-

cence a sign of repentance? Or were they merely attempt-
ing to mollify a prophet they mistakenly believed had the
power to turn away God's wrath?

"I will tell you what the Lord says: My people have forgotten how to do right. Their fortresses are filled with
wealth taken by theft and violence." He saw the subtle
change of expression in some of their faces: a stubborn tilt
of chin, glittering eyes. The hint of rebellion stood all
around him. He did not retreat. "You may fool me with
your words. But do not think you can fool God. He sees
your hearts and knows your inner thoughts. And He will
judge you accordingly."

"Stop your shoving!" someone grumbled.

A man in front of Amos lurched aside as someone
behind him shoved forward. A diminutive man with a
scruffy beard stepped up, ignoring the muttered curses
directed at him. "It would be my honor if you would come
with me, Prophet! I have a booth. You can share it with
me."

"Get out of here, you little weasel, before we skin you
and hang you up on a wall."

The little weasel did not retreat at rough handling. He
fought the hands trying to pull him back and kicked one
man in the shins while shouting at Amos. "What better
place to present your case than in the marketplace? Everyone comes there!" Six to one was no match and he disappeared in the throng, trailed by threats of what might
happen to a man who dared insult a prophet who could
bring on an earthquake.

The elders wanted Amos to talk only to them, but God's
message was for everyone.

Amos looked over the crowd toward the little man. "What's your name?"

"Naharai ben Shagee," the man called from the back of the crowd.

The elders cast dark glances, but it did no good. Naharai's head appeared for an instant at the back; first to the left and then to the right as he jumped up and down in an attempt to see over others' heads.

"Pay him no attention."

"He's no one important."

Amos headed into the crowd. Men moved away from him, afraid, and then closed in behind, squabbling quietly about Naharai's interruption. "Please, stay and talk with us."

Amos found Naharai. "About that booth."

Naharai grinned broadly. "It's right in the middle of the market. A good spot. I will show you." He cast a triumphant look at the men standing in the gate before leading Amos away. "I saw you in the marketplace a few times. You never bought anything."

"What do you sell?" Amos walked alongside him.

"Sandals." He looked down. "You look as though you need a new pair."

Amos cast him a baleful look. "Is it the Word of the Lord you hunger for, or my money?"

"Both!"

Surprised, Amos laughed. *Here, Lord, is an honest man!*

+   +   +

One year passed into another, and then into another. The terror that came with the earthquake waned and people returned to their old ways. And still Amos kept on, teaching and preaching the Word of the Lord, praying constantly that the people would listen and repent.

Every day, Amos taught from the scrolls Beeri had copied and given to him before leaving Bethel. He pored over them, prayed over them, and discussed the Law with anyone who came to him. The Israelites argued over every word of it, turning it this way and that, trying to get out from under the Law. They had wax in their ears and scales over their eyes. Or was it merely their lust for sin that made them deaf and blind to the clarity of God's message?

"Of all the nations and families on the earth," Amos told his small gathering, "He chose us to be His people. The nations have witnessed what the Lord has done for us from the time He sent plagues upon Egypt and delivered us from slavery, then brought us into this land. More recently, the nations have seen how we have forgotten Him."

"You there, Naharai!" A merchant stood over Naharai, hands on hips. "You invited him here, and look how he draws my customers away with all his prattle about law and judgment."

"If your goods were worth anything, customers couldn't be so easily drawn away!"

"Rodent!" He reached for Naharai.

Naharai evaded him easily, and shouted, "Ribai is a cheat! He mixes sand in with his grain."

Some altercation occurred every day, not always at Naharai's booth, but somewhere in the chaos of the marketplace. Yesterday, it had been two women arguing over the price of melons and cucumbers. Today it was the merchant who often sold moldy grain to those who had the least money. Those who walked and talked in awe of their

gods on the temple mount preyed on one another here,
and Ribai was one of the worst.

Amos rose when Ribai caught hold of Naharai. He used
the crook of his staff to prevent a fist from landing.

The merchant swung around, face flushed. "Stay out of
it, Prophet."

"Those who shut their eyes to the cries of the poor will
be ignored by the Lord in their own time of need. To cheat
the poor is to spit in the face of God."

"Mind your own business." Ribai stormed back to his
stall, shouting at his son to watch out for thieves.

"The Lord hears their prayers." Amos returned to his
place and sat. Only a few had come today to hear him read
the Law. The young man who sat waiting only did so until
Naharai could repair his sandals. And a mother had come
with two boys, but left them behind so that she could bar-
ter for trinkets.

Now, another, dressed in fine linen and veils,
approached. She stood listening as Amos read aloud. A
servant held a shade over her while another peeled a
pomegranate. When the slave girl stopped for a moment
to listen intently to him, her mistress pinched her for
neglecting her duties and threatened her with more abuse
if she did not peel the pomegranate more quickly. Spotting
a friend, the woman called her over.

Amos knew them. He had seen them often and been
told by Naharai not to offend them. Wives and daughters
of priests. They strolled through the market, demanding
samples of whatever caught their fancy. And no one dared
refuse. Like fat cows, they grazed continually. No one
dared deny them.

The two whispered while Amos tried to teach. They

laughed low and sneered. Another woman joined them, bejeweled with necklaces and earrings and tinkling brace- lets.

Amos looked up at them. "The life of every living thing is in God's hands, and the breath of all humanity. Remem- ber the Word of the Lord, the Law written down by Moses. If we sin, the Lord will scatter us among the nations. But if we return to Him and obey His command- ments, even if we are exiled to the ends of the earth, the Lord will bring us back to the place He has chosen for His Name to be honored."

Naharai called the young man. He rose quickly, paid for his repaired sandals, and departed, leaving only the two boys who argued and shoved at one another.

Amos ignored them, continuing to address his words to the smug, indolent women who had come out of boredom and only wanted to mock. "You cannot live as you please, breaking God's commandments at every turn, and still expect to receive His blessings."

"In case you hadn't noticed, we already live under God's blessing," one woman said with a derisive laugh.

"God is warning you now. Don't count on your posses- sions to protect you in the coming day. Return to the Lord and the power of His strength."

"Listen to this fool. . . ."

"You should not take whatever you want from the poor, but show compassion and mercy upon them." What would it take to make these people listen? Another earth- quake? Would they try God's patience until the promised disasters came upon them?

The woman used her maid's shawl to wipe pomegranate juice from her hands. "You should have a cup of wine,

Prophet. Perhaps then you would not be so filled with gloom." She tossed the shawl heedlessly aside.

"Always the same speech." Her friend shrugged. "He never speaks of anything pleasurable."

"A visit to the temple brothel would put him in better spirits."

The women laughed together.

The first woman waved her hand airily at the two boys. "Don't listen to him, my fine young fellows. What he wants to do is take all the pleasure from our lives and make us reunite with Judah. We don't need Judah."

Fire spread through Amos's blood. "You fat cows! Keep fattening yourselves for the slaughter."

Red-faced, the woman shoved her maid aside and stepped forward. "What did you call me?"

"You heard me." Amos rose, his eyes fixing upon the three women. "You're fed on the finest grains, tended with the greatest care, and for what? One day you will lose everything you value, including your life!"

"You don't know who I am!"

"I know who you are. And I know your kind." He had had sheep like them, butting the younger ones, bullying. Greedy, possessive, danger to the flock. If not dealt with, they led others astray.

Naharai shook his head at Amos and mouthed, *Don't say any more.*

But Amos had to continue. If he did not speak the truth to these women, their blood would be on his conscience. These women walked about on the temple mount, heads held high because their husbands served as priests or officials. He saw them here often, extorting whatever they wanted at the expense of those far less fortunate than they. "You are women who oppress the poor and crush the needy, and who are always calling to your husbands, 'Bring us another drink!'"

"A wiser man would keep his mouth shut!"

One of them sang a mocking tune, one that had grown common over the past months.

The Word of the Lord came in a hot rush from Amos's lips. "The Sovereign Lord has sworn this by His holiness!" He pointed at the women mocking him. "'The time will come when you will be led away with hooks in your noses. Every last one of you will be dragged away like a fish on a hook! You will be led out through the ruins of the wall; you will be thrown from your fortresses,' says the Lord. 'And I will destroy the beautiful homes of the wealthy—their winter mansions and their summer houses, too—all their palaces filled with ivory.'"

Face flushed red in anger, the first woman cried out. "I worship God! I'm at the temple every morning, and I bring generous offerings."

"Stolen offerings to a false god!"

Others in the marketplace paused to stare. Naharai ducked back into his booth and hid in the back.

Amos came toward the women. "Go ahead and offer your sacrifices to the idols. See if they can help when your enemies breach the walls. Keep on disobeying. Your sins are mounting up."

She sputtered while her friends closed in.

"Come away."

"Don't listen to him."

"He's mad. Just ignore him."

"A curse on you, Prophet!"

As they walked away, Amos shouted, "Prepare to meet your God!"

"He's not my god!" she shrieked back at him.

The others put their arms around her and drew her away.

Amos shook his head. "Fools are wise in their own eyes, but the Lord prevails." He took his place again and looked at the two boys, now silent, big-eyed, watching him. Only three others remained.

"You'll be sorry, Amos."

"More sorry if I had held my tongue."

One of the men did not understand. "Why has the Lord not spoken to us before now?"

Stifling his impatience, Amos leaned forward. "He has spoken to the ten tribes many times. He sent famine to every town and kept the rain from falling to make us turn back. He struck farms and vineyards with blight and mildew. He even sent plagues like the ones He sent against Egypt. Our young men died in wars, and some cities were destroyed. The Lord told us these things would happen if we turned our backs on Him. The Lord is the one who shaped the mountains. He stirs the winds and reveals every thought of man. He turns the light of dawn into darkness."

"But what God asks of us is too complicated!"

"The command God gave us through Moses is not too difficult for you to understand, and it is not beyond your reach. It is not kept in heaven, so distant that you must ask, 'Who will go up to heaven and bring it down so we can hear it and obey?' It is not kept beyond the sea, so far away that you must ask, 'Who will cross the sea to bring it to us so we can hear it and obey?' No, the message is very close at hand; it is on your lips and in your heart so that you can obey it. God gave us a choice between life and death, between prosperity and disaster. But you have allowed your hearts to be drawn away from Him to worship other gods.

"Listen! He is the Lord our God. You must not have any other god but Him. You must not make for yourself an idol of any kind. You must not misuse the name of the Lord your God. Remember to observe the Sabbath day by keeping it holy. Honor your father and mother. You must not murder. You must not commit adultery. You must not steal. You must not testify falsely against your neighbor. You must not covet anything that belongs to your neighbor."

"Why can't we worship the Lord and other gods, too?"

"Because the Lord God is One! There is no other god."

One of the men rose. "I don't believe that. I won't believe it." He walked away.

Amos spoke intently to the few who remained. "Return to the Lord and live. Don't go to worship the idols of Bethel, Gilgal, or Beersheba. For the people of Gilgal will be dragged off into exile as well, and the people of Bethel will come to nothing!"

"Life doesn't have to be so hard. Look around you, Amos. We have wealth on every side. The famines are over. We have food enough to grow fat like the cows of Bashan." The man stood. "No one will slaughter us, because King Jeroboam has assembled and equipped an army so that we can stand against anyone."

Nothing Amos said seemed to sink in. He might as well have been pouring water into sand. These people had lost the knowledge of their foundation. Ignorance would bring them to destruction. But they did not have hearts soft enough to be molded by God's Word. They were hard and proud, putting their confidence in the wealth and power of their king and country.

Another man stood. "Even if I believed—which I can't because of all I see around me—I would be one of few who followed your teachings." He shook his head. "But we're free here. We are not bound by your laws. Life is to be lived. It is to be enjoyed."

Free to sin, he meant. Angry, frustrated, anguished, Amos cried out. "You cannot stand against God. He takes away the understanding of kings, and He leaves them wandering in a wasteland without a path."

The man's face grew rigid with defiance. "You said all blessings come from the Lord, but the truth is God didn't give us any of what we have! Jeroboam, the son of Nebat, gave Israel freedom and prosperity. He removed Solomon's yoke from our necks!"

"And put on the yoke of sin, which will lead you to death."

Angry, the young man lashed out. "We are stronger than you think! You are a blind prophet, so you can't see that. And why shouldn't we be proud? The dynasty of Jeroboam has grown more powerful each year. We hold our land. Our borders are expanding. Samaria is a greater capital city than Jerusalem!"

"Israel will answer to God."

"So you keep saying. Year after year, you say the same thing and nothing happens! It is you who must learn, Prophet. You have nothing to offer our people. You're a fool, Amos. You speak from madness, not wisdom."

"Only by the power of God can we push back our enemies; only in His name can we trample our foes."

"Then how did all this come to be after we broke away from the rulers in Jerusalem!"

"God is patient. He—"

"Patient? Your god is *weak*. I prefer bowing down to a god with power!"

"The one who toppled during the earthquake? The one who broke the horns off his own altar as he fell? That's the god you think has power?"

The young man's eyes flickered, and then darkened. "A curse on your prophecies. A curse on you!" Turning his back, he walked away.

Others who had watched and listened, clapped and cheered. Again, Amos heard taunting.

Lord, You have shot an arrow into my heart. All day long these people sing their mocking songs.

Amos struggled with anger and grief. Words rose in his throat, but they were not from God, and he swallowed them, clenching his teeth to keep from sinning. "The Lord does not enjoy hurting people or causing them sorrow. Repent! Accept His discipline when it comes. Return to the Lord. Hear, O Israel! The Lord is One. Love the Lord your God with all your heart, all your soul, and all your strength. . . ."

The people turned away.

Amos's eyes grew hot with tears. "If we will humble ourselves and pray and seek God's face and turn from our wicked ways, the Lord will hear from heaven and will forgive our sins and restore our land. If we do not repent and return to Him, the Lord has said Philistia and Egypt will sit around the hills of Samaria and witness what punishment He will bring upon us for our sins."

No one listened.

+   +   +

Naharai drew the flap down on his booth and came to sit with Amos. "This was a very bad day." He rubbed his hands.

Amos read the signs. "What troubles you, Naharai?" He knew already, but hoped having to voice it would cause Naharai to think longer.

"You used to draw crowds. Everyone wanted to hear what you had to say."

Because the earthquake had aroused the fear of the Lord in them. Within a year, though, it had lessened. Now, it was all but forgotten.

Naharai rubbed his palms over his tunic-covered knees and left damp spots. "The people don't want to listen to you anymore, Amos." He shook his head. "Three years ago—even a year—and I would not worry, but times have changed. Despite what you claim, no one believes God had anything to do with the earthquake. It just . . . happened."

Amos said nothing, but his heart broke. Even Naharai was deaf to the Word of the Lord. "Even after all this time, and hearing everything I have said, you fail to believe that God will bring judgment upon Israel."

"Why would anyone want to believe such a thing, Amos? Even if they did believe it, wouldn't that be all the more reason to eat, drink, and be merry? If death is coming and there is no way to stop it, then we must take all the pleasure we can now."

"Repentance—"

Naharai waved his hands impatiently. "Yes, yes, you've said that word a thousand times. It rubs men raw."

"Not raw enough."

"You should respect me more."

"What are you talking about?" Amos stared at Naharai in confusion.

"I tried to warn you not to insult those women today, but you ignored me." He pointed to himself. "Me! The one who gave you the use of this booth."

Amos had never been fooled by Naharai's generosity. The merchant's motives had always been selfish. "You made this booth so that I would draw a crowd and you could sell your sandals."

Naharai's eyes flashed. "Even so, you should thank me. Instead, you cause trouble. Did you have a single thought for me or my business when you insulted those women? Fat cows, you called them!"

"And so they are."

"No! Say no more! Not another word! You've said too much already. You never think of the consequences, do you? You just keep pointing your finger, making accusations, and pretending you know everything that will happen." He stood. "You are bad for business, and I want you to go away. *Now!*"

Amos stared at him. He had hoped to reach these people, and had not reached even one. Naharai had boasted once that he did not bow down to a golden calf. True enough. He had never given up bowing down to profits.

Weary, Amos took his staff. He looked long at Naharai. "I had hoped . . ." Tears welled in his eyes. Shaking his head, he walked away.

Naharai called after him. "I like you, Amos." His tone filled with uneasiness. "I mean no disrespect to you or your God, but a man has to make a living."

"You have chosen, Naharai."

One day, sooner than he thought, death would be at his door.

✦   ✦   ✦

As Amos walked through the streets of Bethel, he looked into the faces of the people. Despite their sins, he had come to love them. They were like a flock of sheep, dumb and prone to wander, ignorant of the dangers that lurked everywhere, oblivious to the enemy Satan who longed to devour them. They followed their desires, foraging in foreign religions that fanned their pride and base passions. They thought they could live without God's rules and made up rules of their own. They couldn't seem to understand that every man cannot live for himself without bringing chaos. The very things they longed for were within reach if only they would return to God.

The love God offered each of them would fulfill the longing of their souls, while the love offered in the temple of Bethel would leave them empty and diseased. The freedom God offered would build them up and give them purpose while the freedom offered by idols would captivate and enslave them. They wanted fair treatment and would have it if they obeyed the law of God. Instead, they bowed down to man-made rules that gave corrupt men power to grind the poor beneath their heels and grow rich upon others' labors.

Their hearts were like stone, impenetrable. They wore the armor of pride.

Anguish filled Amos. He had seen their end. Crying out, he wept and tore his robe. "Come, let us tell of the Lord's greatness; let us exalt His name together. I prayed to the Lord, and He answered me. He freed me from all my fears. Those who look to Him for help will be radiant with joy; no shadow of shame will darken their faces. The Lord will set us free from fear!"

His words fell on deaf ears, for they had lost their fear of the Lord. Earthquakes came and shook their confidence. But when the rubble was cleared away, the warning was forgotten and they returned to their old ways.

"Listen, you people of Israel!" Amos cried in anguish. "Listen to this funeral song I am singing!" His voice rose in a sad lament to the virgin Israel's fall from grace, never to rise again. He sang of her lying abandoned on the ground with no one to help her up.

People came out of their houses, peered down from their windows, paused in their work to listen, for his voice was like that of the Lord, beautiful and terrible at the same time. His song echoed in the gates and then drifted on the wind as he left the city and walked slowly, shoulders slumped, to his cave.

And the people talked among themselves.

"I hope he never comes back."

"I wish he would go away."

"Someone should go out there and shut him up for good."

"He never has anything good to say to us."

"Doom and gloom. That's all he's about."

"All he ever does is tell us what he thinks we're doing wrong."

Amos sat inside his cave, head in his hands, shoulders

shaking with sobs. "Oh, Lord, oh, Lord. Turn their hearts to soft clay. Please, Lord . . ."

But he already knew the answer. The people had turned away. Their hearts were hardened.

And God was storing up wrath for the day to come.

SIX

AMOS walked the hills. He looked out over the land. Bethel stood proud in the distance.

Why are Your people so stubborn, Lord?

Why do they turn privilege into perversion? They don't even know right from wrong anymore. Their homes are filled with possessions they've stolen from others. Looters! That's what they are. Thieves and brigands. Godless women. Hypocrites. They laugh at me when I warn them of what will happen to them. They refuse to believe Your Word. You, the Living God who created heaven and earth. How can they be so foolish as to think their idols can save them?

Amos rubbed his face in disappointment. He had failed. Nothing he had said had made any difference in the way they lived.

Maybe if he had been a more learned man, or more eloquent or forceful or persuasive in his speech, they might have listened.

How long, O Lord, You have weighed me down with love for these people. How long must I stay and see how they turn their backs on You? I am crushed by their sins, burdened by their complaints, awash with tears over their rebellion! When will You let me go home?

God had given them opportunity after opportunity to turn away from their false gods and pagan worship. *Repentance* was a foul word in their mouths. "Repent of what?" they said, convinced their wealth would save them. They called for the Day of the Lord to come and had no idea that when it came it would sweep over them and blow them away like chaff before the wind.

They're like children, Amos thought, *holding Your hand while plotting mischief. They think You'll do nothing to them because You chose them out of all the people of the earth as Your possession. But will a father ignore the disrespect of his children? Will he allow his children to spit in his face? If a human father will not allow it, why should they think the Lord God will?*

Shoulders heaving, he sobbed. He had told them the truth and been reviled. And they went on trampling the poor among them. Their leaders continued to extort bribes and repress justice. Many grew lazy and complacent, lounging in luxury, indulging themselves on choice meat, and singing songs about nothing. "Let's eat, drink, and be merry," they said to one another, thinking God would not hold them accountable because they were sons of Jacob. To them, Jehovah was just another god among their pantheon, and the least favorite because the Lord God of Israel called for holy living and self-sacrifice for the sake of others. And because of their rejection, their hearts grew harder, their ears deafer. They didn't know truth from lies.

"I've told them, Lord. I've told them and told them."

Those who tried to live righteous lives before God suffered. Beeri, Jerusha, and Hosea had gone back to Jerusalem. Amos hoped they had found others who loved the Lord as they did, who clung to the Torah for wisdom and guidance, who lived to please not men, but God.

Grief and anger filled Amos. He felt torn between loving and hating the people of Bethel.

It is not you they have rejected, Amos. They have rejected Me.

"But, Lord, they don't understand that they are going to get what they deserve! They will get exactly what they're asking for: the Day of the Lord. It will come upon them sooner than they think."

Rather than be victors over their enemies, they would be broken and deserted. The ten tribes would fall, never to rise again. Nine out of ten of their soldiers would die in battle, the rest enslaved. Weeping would be heard everywhere, and still things would go from bad to worse. The Day of the Lord would be a day without a single ray of hope. All their worship would end. Their songs would be silenced. Those who survived the battles would be led away as slaves, their pride and the glory that was Israel obliterated, all their wealth in the hands of their enemies.

Amos knelt, head to the ground. "What do I do, Lord? What do I say to them to turn them away from destruction?"

Stand firm! Continue to tell them the truth!

Colors changed around him. He felt God's presence enveloping him, comforting while showing him the future. He saw locusts come up out of the ground, vast numbers of them, like an army of millions upon millions, marching, spreading across the land, taking flight. Everything in their path disappeared. The land became a black sea of moving insects gorging on crops, trees, brush, even people.

"O Sovereign Lord!" Amos cried out, hands raised. "Please forgive us or we will not survive, for Israel is so small."

The vision disappeared.

I will not do it.

Even as Amos thanked God for not obliterating the land and people, another vision filled his mind. Scorching heat bubbled in the bottom of the ocean, sending clouds of steam into the air. Fire raged from the mountainous depths of the sea, rising, rising, a cauldron of bubbles and steam, spreading and devouring the entire land.

"God, no!" Amos cried out in fear. "O Sovereign Lord, please stop or we will not survive, for Israel is so small."

The Lord spoke in a still, quiet voice:

I will not do that, either.

The fire disappeared and the land was as it had been.

Amos's heart pounded, for the Lord was not finished showing His great power over all creation. Discipline would come. It must come to turn His people back. Amos prayed for mercy upon them. "Leave a remnant, Lord. Please, leave someone alive to praise Your Name."

Amos, what do you see?

Amos opened his eyes. "A plumb line." The Law was the weight on the end of it.

I will test My people with this plumb line. I will no longer ignore all their sins. The pagan shrines of your ancestors will be ruined, and the temples of Israel will be destroyed; I will bring the dynasty of King Jeroboam to a sudden end. Go and tell them!

Ten tribes had aligned themselves with the pagan gods of Canaan, Moab, Ammon, and the rest. Not one in all Israel would stand straight and true beside the law Moses

had brought down from Mount Sinai, the law God had
written in His own hand.

How could they not see that God pursued them with
relentless love? How could they not respond?

Burdened by sorrow, Amos headed back to Bethel.

The people had refused to heed the Lord's warning.
They had planted the wind; now, they would harvest the
whirlwind of a righteous, holy God.

✦   ✦   ✦

Amos knew as he approached the temple that his time
was short. Already, men ran up the steps to report his
presence.

"Listen to the Word of the Lord!" he shouted. "Recite
My law no longer, and don't pretend that you obey Me.
You refuse My discipline and treat My laws like trash!" He
listed all their sins, despite catcalls, mock bows, shouted
curses, and insults. "Your mouths are filled with wicked-
ness, and your tongues full of lies. While you did all this,
I remained silent, and you thought I didn't care! But now
I will rebuke you!"

"He's speaking against the king!"

A commotion started above and behind him. The temple guards ran down the steps and surrounded him. "You
are ordered to be silent!"

"Repent!"

"Shut up!" Two guards with swords took hold of him.

Amos struggled. "Repent, all of you who ignore the
Lord, or He will tear you apart, and no one will help you!"

The guards grappled with him. When he tried to use his
staff, two guards wrenched it from his hand.

"Silence him!"

The guards struck him with his own staff. Stunned by
the blows, Amos sagged. Guards grabbed him, hauling
him up and half carried, half dragged him up the steps.
The air chilled inside the temple. He was brought into a
large chamber and dropped on the stone floor. He groaned
and tried to get up. A guard kicked him. The others joined
in. Pain shot through him. He could hardly breathe.

"Enough!"

"What do you want done with him, my lord?"

My lord. Wrath filled Amos, and he struggled to his feet
and faced Amaziah. "There is no other Lord but Jehovah."

The high priest's eyes blackened with hatred. "For ten
years I've suffered your presence in my city, but no more.
Finally, you have gone too far. No one is permitted to
prophesy against the king!"

"It was the Lord who gave ten tribes to Jeroboam, and
what did Jeroboam do to show his gratitude?" Amos
sneered. "He set up golden calves and led the people away
from the God who blessed him. *Jeroboam's dynasty will
come to an end!*" Struck again, Amos fell. He raised his
head with an effort. "The Lord has spoken."

"The king will hear your words, Amos. Then you will
die."

"Tell him!" Amos struggled with all his strength, but
could not gain freedom. "Tell him what the Lord says. If
he has any sense, he will repent and lead his people back
to God."

"Lock him away!"

✦   ✦   ✦

Heaved into darkness, the door closed and barred behind
him, Amos lay facedown on the cold earth. The stench of

the fetid palace underworld made his head swim and his
stomach heave. A rat scrambled up his leg. He drew back
and hit it away. Squeaking, it scurried away to wait for a
more opportune time.

Fear gripped Amos by the throat. Never had he been in
such darkness. Always there had been the stars overhead.
But this blackness had teeth that sank into his soul. He
fought to keep from screaming and felt the walls for a way
out. There was none.

"God, help me." Even his whisper echoed softly.

Sinking down, he pressed his back against the wall. He
strained to see even a small flicker of light—somewhere,
anywhere. Nothing. Only by closing his eyes could he
imagine it. A man used to open spaces and the sheepfold,
Amos fought against panic with prayer.

"Lord, You are my deliverer. Blow them away like chaff
in the wind—a wind sent by the angel of the Lord. Make
their path dark and slippery, with the angel of the Lord
pursuing them. Although I did them no wrong, they laid a
trap for me. Although I did them no wrong, they dug a pit
for me. So let sudden ruin overtake them. Let them be
caught in their own snares!"

Time passed slowly, but Amos kept his thoughts fixed
upon the Lord. He shouted God's Word into the darkness.
"Return to the Lord! Giving thanks is a sacrifice that truly
honors Him. If you keep to His path, He will reveal to you
the salvation of God!" Anger filled him. "The wicked plots
against the righteous and gnashes his teeth at him. The
Lord laughs at him, for He sees his day is coming!"

A guard raged, "Will you never learn to hold your
tongue, Prophet? When the order comes, it will please me
to cut it out!"

He was given only enough food and water to keep him alive. Standing in the darkness of his prison, he wailed over the fate of the people. "This is what the Lord says: 'From among all the families on the earth, I chose you alone. That is why I must punish you for all your sins. Listen, all the earth! I will bring disaster upon My people. It is the fruit of their own sin because they refuse to listen to Me!'"

"Shut up!"

"You boast that you are more powerful than any other nation! You think you can dodge the grave. You say the Assyrians can never touch you, for you've made strong towers. Hear, O Israel! You live in a refuge made of lies and deception!"

More guards entered. The torchlight was so bright it blinded him. They cursed him, punched him, and kicked him until he lost consciousness.

When he awakened in darkness, he crawled into a corner and prayed. "Lord, deliver me. . ."

✦   ✦   ✦

The door opened to a shout of, "Get up!" When he couldn't, two guards grabbed hold of him and pulled him up, uncaring of his pain. "You stink, Prophet."

He was brought upstairs and outside.

The sunlight hurt his eyes and blinded him. *Is this the way it is for these people, Lord? They close their eyes to the light of truth because it is too painful to accept? It will mean they have to change their ways!*

How long had he been imprisoned? A week? A month? He filled his lungs with clean air.

Amos found himself standing before Paarai, Amaziah's

son. Attired in the garb of a priest—jeweled with insignias of his office—he held his head high. Lip curled, he surveyed Amos with cold eyes. "The king has been informed of the plots you've tried to hatch against him."

"Lies! I have hatched no plots."

A guard struck him. He was dragged up again before the high priest's son.

"We have witnesses. Right here in Bethel, on the doorstep of King Jeroboam's royal sanctuary, you spoke of a plot to end his life and destroy his dynasty. You said he would soon be killed, and the people of Israel sent away into exile."

You said . . . you said . . . Amos understood. "Jeroboam's dynasty shall end. Yes. Not my words, but the Lord's."

Eyes hot, face flushed, Paarai shouted at him. "Hear the word of my father, Amaziah, high priest of Bethel and servant of Baal! Get out of here, you prophet! Go on back to the land of Judah, and earn your living by prophesying there! Don't bother us with your prophecies here in Bethel. This is the king's sanctuary and the national place of worship!"

Amos knew Amaziah was somewhere close, listening. "I'm not a professional prophet, not like you and your father and others like you who speak whatever is pleasing to the ear of the one who pays you! I was never trained to be a prophet. I'm just a shepherd, and I take care of sycamore-fig trees. But the Lord called me away from my flock and told me, 'Go and prophesy to My people in Israel!'"

Amaziah entered the room. Face mottled, he spat out words of hatred. "Get him out of my sight! He is banished from Bethel. See that no one allows him in the gate again!"

"What's the matter, Amaziah? Did Jeroboam defeat your plan to kill me? Is there a residue of fear of the Lord left in Israel? Pray it is so!"

"Let the people see him banished, Father."

"So be it!" Amaziah agreed.

The Spirit of the Lord came upon Amos in power, and he cried out in a loud voice. "Now then, listen to this message from the Lord, Amaziah. You say, 'Don't prophesy against Israel. Stop preaching against My people.' But this is what the Lord says: 'Your wife will become a prostitute in this city, and your sons and daughters will be killed. Your land will be divided up, and you yourself will die in a foreign land. And the people of Israel will certainly become captives in exile, far from their homeland.'"

Gagging him, the guards took him outside, whipped him, and tied him in an oxcart. They paraded him through the streets of Bethel. People shouted insults and curses.

"What of your prophecies now, Prophet?"

Some laughed.

"Out of our way!" the temple guard shouted.

"Get him out of here!"

Some threw refuse.

"Send him home to Judah!"

The oxcart took him into the shadow of the gate and then out into the sunlight where the guards released him.

Half-starved, beaten, Amos could barely stand. He pointed to those shouting down at him from the walls. "You will become captives in exile, far from your homeland."

No one heard him.

No one cared enough to listen.

✦ ✦ ✦

Amos dreamed that night, a waking dream as he walked beneath the stars.

What do you see, Amos?

"A basket full of ripe fruit." Fruit ready to be eaten.

The ten tribes were ripe for punishment. The singing in the temples of Israel would turn to wailing. Dead bodies would be scattered everywhere. The survivors would be taken out of the city in silence. The ten wayward tribes would be led away into slavery. Even the land would suffer because of them.

Israel first.

Then Judah.

Wailing, Amos sank to his knees and threw dust in the air. He raged against the people's sins and grieved through the night. In the morning, he got up from the dust and walked back to Bethel.

"You can't come in, Prophet. You heard the orders yesterday."

"These walls will not protect you from the judgment of God!"

"Go away! Don't make trouble for me."

"Listen to the message that the Lord has spoken!" Amos shouted up at the people on the wall. "Listen to this, you who rob the poor and trample down the needy! You can't wait for the Sabbath day to be over and the religious festivals to end so you can get back to cheating the helpless."

All day, Amos walked along the walls of Bethel. "The Day of the Lord will come unexpectedly, like a thief in the night! 'In that day,' says the Sovereign Lord, 'I will make the sun go down at noon and darken the earth while it is still day. I will turn your celebrations into times of mourning and your singing into weeping. You will wear funeral clothes and shave your heads to show your sorrow—as if your only son had died. How very bitter that day will be!'"

Throat raw, Amos stared up at the walls. Tears ran down his cheeks at the thought of the destruction to come.

The Spirit of the Lord renewed his strength and gave power to his voice as he warned them of the worst curse that could come upon man. "'The time is surely coming,' says the Sovereign Lord, 'when I will send a famine on the land—not a famine of bread or water but of hearing the Words of the Lord.'" Sobbing, Amos tore his robes. "People will stagger from sea to sea and wander from border to border searching for the Word of the Lord, but they will not find it. Beautiful girls and strong young men will grow faint in that day, thirsting for the Lord's Word."

He pointed to the people lining the walls on either side of the main gates. "And those who swear by the shameful idols of Samaria—who take oaths in the name of the god of Dan and make vows in the name of the god of Beersheeba—they will all fall down, never to rise again."

A rock struck him in the forehead and he fell. Blood poured down his face. He wiped it away and pushed himself up. Another stone and another. Pain licked through his shoulder and side.

Amos backed away from the walls. "'Are you Israelites more important to Me than the Ethiopians?' asks the Lord. 'I brought Israel out of Egypt, but I also brought the Philistines from Crete and led the Arameans out of Kir.

I, the Sovereign Lord, am watching this sinful nation of Israel. I will destroy it from the face of the earth!'"

Amaziah stood in the shadows shouting, "We will not listen to you any longer! Close the gate!"

The merchants protested; he could hear them arguing. No one cared about hearing the Word of the Lord—they only fought to reopen the gates so that commerce could continue!

Amos turned away, head throbbing, and staggered down the hill. Coming at last to a quiet orchard, he collapsed.

✦   ✦   ✦

Awakening in the middle of the night, Amos managed to make his way to the sheepfold cave where he had lived for ten years. Hungry and thirsty, he fell on the hard-packed earth and curled up like a babe in the womb. Would he die here like an animal in its hole?

"Lord, why have You abandoned me? I tried to feed Your sheep. They would not partake." Broken in spirit, he sobbed. Throat raw and lips cracked and bleeding, he whispered, "You are God and there is no other. Blessed be the Name of the Lord."

He dreamed that angels came and gave him bread and water while God whispered to him like a father to a troubled child.

Be still, and know that I AM God.

The pain went away and Amos's body relaxed beneath the ministering hands. "Abba . . . Abba . . . they wouldn't listen." He heard weeping.

Release came, and another task with freedom.

Tomorrow, he would go home to Tekoa, and write all the visions the Lord had given him. He would make a copy for Israel and another for Judah. The indictment would be on scrolls so that when the Lord fulfilled His Word, the people would know He had warned them before sending His judgment.

✦   ✦   ✦

The eleven miles to Tekoa felt like one hundred, but the sight of the fields and flocks of sheep filled Amos with joy. He spotted Elkanan and Ithai in the pastures, but could not raise his arm or call out to them.

Elkanan studied him.

Ithai approached, staff and club in hand. "You there! Who are you and what do you want?"

Had he changed so much in appearance? Swaying, Amos dropped to his knees.

Ithai hurried toward him. When Amos lifted his head, Ithai's eyes went wide. "Uncle!" Dropping his club, he put his arm around him. "Let me help you." He shouted, "Elkanan! It's Uncle Amos! Call for help!"

"I will be all right. I just need to rest here awhile." When Amos looked out at the sheep, his throat closed, hot and thick. Why couldn't Israel be drawn together and led back to the Lord? Why couldn't they graze on the Scriptures rather than eat the poisonous teachings of men like Jeroboam, Amaziah . . . Heled?

"Amos is back!"

"Hush." Amos shook his head. "Don't frighten the sheep." His voice broke. *If only God's sheep were frightened of what was to come. If only they could be called back. . . .*

Others came to help. Eliakim reached for him, tears running freely as he looped his arm gently around Amos and helped him walk.

Amos smiled. "My friend, I need you to purchase reed pens, a full inkhorn, a small knife, and a roll of papyrus right away."

"I will, Amos."

✦   ✦   ✦

Amos slept for three days.

Finally he rose, stiff and aching, and set to work on the scroll. The Word of the Lord flowed from him, the Spirit of the Lord helping him to remember every word God had spoken. When his emotions rose too high, he left the work briefly and paced so that his tears would not stain the document.

Eliakim set down a tray with a jug of wine, some bread, and a bowl of thick lentil stew. "You must eat."

Amos did so. Replete, he returned to his work.

Eliakim came to get the tray and bowl. "Will the Lord send you back to Israel?"

"I don't know." He was not the same man who had left Tekoa years ago. "I will go wherever God sends me." His heart still ached for the Israelites.

"Much has changed in Jerusalem since the earthquake. Uzziah lives in solitude. Jotham carries out his commands."

"Did the king repent?"

"Yes."

"And the people?" He thought of his brothers, their wives and young ones. "Have they returned to the Lord?"

"Many have."

His servant's hesitance grieved Amos. "My brothers
. . ."

Eliakim shrugged. "It appears so."

Out of obligation or thanksgiving? Amos had not the
heart to ask. He prayed that his brothers bowed down
willingly to the Lord and could rejoice in their salvation.

He worked day by day, carefully writing the first
scroll. There must be no mistakes. When he finished writing the visions, the Lord spoke to him again, and the
Word He gave filled Amos with hope for those who
trusted in the Lord.

He finished writing, left the table, and went outside.
Raising his arms in praise to the God who had called him
away from the fields and flocks, he thought of the future
and hope God offered His people.

"In that day I will restore the fallen house of David.
I will repair its damaged walls. From the ruins I will
rebuild it and restore its former glory. I will bring My
exiled people of Israel back from distant lands, and they
will rebuild their ruined cities and live in them again.
They will plant vineyards and gardens; they will eat their
crops and drink their wine. I will firmly plant them there
in their own land."

All would not be lost. God always left a remnant.

Amos went back to his writing table, and over the next
weeks made two perfect copies of the scroll. The first he
sent by messenger to King Jeroboam in Samaria, the second to King Uzziah in Jerusalem, and the third he placed
in Eliakim's trustworthy hands. "Keep this safe lest the
others be destroyed." Some men would do anything to
pretend God did not speak or warn of what was to come.

His work done, Amos went out to examine the flocks.

He saw the increase that had come from Elkanan's and Ithai's care over the last ten years and was pleased.

✦   ✦   ✦

Much had changed during his absence, and dismayed, Amos had to accept that his sheep no longer recognized his voice. The lamb he had tended had grown old. The animals moved at the sound of Elkanan's and Ithai's voices, but they did not come when Amos called. Like the Israelites, they had forgotten their master's voice. They no longer knew or trusted him. Working with his nephews, Amos allowed the animals time to become familiar with his voice.

When they finally answered to his voice, he took a portion of the flock to another pasture. He walked among them and talked softly to them. Some inclined their ears, others did not. At night, with the howl of wolves, he played his reed pipe or sang to them. The sound of his presence helped the sheep rest while keeping predators away.

Even after weeks away from Bethel, he often thought of the people there and what the future held for them. *Should I go back, Lord? Should I try again? How like wayward sheep they are! They don't know Your voice or see Your presence all around them.*

The ten tribes did not know God was close, ever watchful, trying to protect them from harm. They rejected the gift of salvation. They refused to be led to safety, rejecting an abundance of love, joy, peace, patience, kindness, goodness, faithfulness, gentleness, and self-control. Against such things there is no law. Did they even guess at the sorrow they caused God by their adultery with

other gods, gods empty and false, mere reflections of their
own inner depravity? Their false gods would lead them
to slavery and death.

Amos prayed unceasingly. Every thought that came
into his mind he captured and turned to the Lord. He
wanted to be cleansed of all the iniquity he had seen in
Bethel, the sins that had spread through the ten tribes like
a plague. Death would come when they least expected it,
like a thief in the night.

He grieved over Judah, too, for he had returned to
Jerusalem and seen his brothers. And he knew their
repentance did not run deep. Amos prayed for Isaiah's
words to echo through the land and turn the people away
from sin.

Make them listen, Lord!

He brought his flock back to the fold in Tekoa.

Eliakim came out to help him. "King Jeroboam is dead."

Amos heard the news in silence. Dread filled him. *So it
begins.*

Eliakim told him the rest. "His son Zechariah is to rule."

The last sheep entered the fold. Amos closed the gate
securely and bowed his head in grief. "Not for long."

✦   ✦   ✦

The next morning, Amos led his sheep out the gate and
into the east pasture. Leaning on his staff, he watched the
rams and ewes rush to fresh grasses while the lambs
cavorted playfully. He smiled. This was the life he knew
best, the life he loved. He knew sheep, but he could never
fathom men. He thought of Bethel and Israel and prayed
for the people who had persecuted him.

How little pleasure You get from Your flock, Lord. You cry

*out for Your lost children to come home, only to have them
run in the opposite direction.*

Often Amos's sheep wandered. Did that mean he loved
them less? Did it mean he would turn his back on them if
there was any chance to save them?

I am but a man, thought Amos, *and I love them until my
heart feels as though it will break. How much greater is Your
love. It runs deeper, is more pure, is holy. Your love runs like
living water unseen, beyond comprehension, beneath the sur-
face of what we see and hear. Faith stretches toward it and
drinks and drinks so that we might grow strong and upright,
a tree of life to all of us.*

"Amos!"

Startled, Amos straightened and glanced up. The sheep
moved, frightened by the stranger among them. Amos
called them back and moved between the flock and the
man approaching. Grinning, he spread his arms. "Hosea!"

They embraced. Hosea drew back. "I went to Tekoa.
Your servant said you would be here."

"You came five miles to see me?"

"I would have walked farther."

Touched, Amos leaned on his staff and smiled faintly.
"You look well and prosperous."

Hosea bowed his head. "The Lord has blessed our family. My father is performing priestly duties and receives
his portion."

"Ah, yes. And all it took was an earthquake to make
men turn their eyes back to the law of God." He saw this
was no idle visit. "What brings you to me?"

"God has called me back to Israel, Amos."

"Now?"

"Yes."

Amos sighed heavily. "I hope you will find listening ears and open hearts, my young friend."

Hosea bowed his head. "God has told me to marry a prostitute."

Amos stared at him. "Are you certain God is the one speaking to you?"

Hosea lifted his eyes. "When you were called, was there any doubt in your mind that it was God who spoke to you?"

"No. I knew His voice instantly though I had never heard it before. Everything within me recognized Him." Amos gave a faint smile. "I did not welcome Him. I begged Him to leave me alone. I feared the task. I told Him I would not be up to it." He looked north. "And I wasn't." The grief welled again, deep as an ocean. "They refused to listen."

"You spoke the truth, Amos. You warned them of the destruction coming, and now, God is sending me back to live a life filled with pain." Hosea's shoulders sagged. "My father thinks I yearn for Israel's ways. He thinks I want to return to Bethel so I can revel in the pleasure of women! He refuses to speak to me, Amos. I have never lain with a woman. Never! I have waited in hope of finding a God-fearing Hebrew girl who would be the mother of my children." His eyes filled. "And now God tells me to go and marry a prostitute. How can I love such a woman? How can she love me?"

"What else did God say to you?"

He swallowed hard and looked away. He remained silent so long, Amos thought he would not answer. "Israel is like an unfaithful wife. But God is ever faithful. As I must be."

Is this the way of it, Lord? Hosea will be the faithful husband to the adulterous wife, the husband who cherishes his bride, only to see her run to other men. What suffering this young man will experience! And all to show God's anguish. Hosea will show them how You suffer when Your people embrace other gods.

Will the people even know what they see, Lord? Will they understand the depth of Your passion for them? Fear did not turn them back to You. Will love do what fear could not?

You extend Your hand yet again, Lord.

For just a moment, Amos felt God's anguish over His chosen people.

"I don't want to go back to Bethel, Amos. I want to stay in Jerusalem and immerse myself in the study of the Law."

"And you think you will be safe from harm there?" Amos shook his head.

Hosea struggled as he had. Wasn't every day a struggle to obey God rather than do as he pleased? "The only safe place is in God's will, my friend." He put his hand on Hosea's shoulder. "And the Lord is with you. That is worth everything. Perhaps we are all called to be like Job and be able to speak his words from our hearts: 'God might kill me, but I have no other hope.'" *But doesn't the Lord suffer all the more? He loves us like a father loves a child, only more so.*

They walked together. Amos told him the way of a shepherd and pointed out the different sheep and their personalities. Hosea laughed and shook his head. And it occurred to Amos as he was instructing Hosea that all of creation taught about the character of God. Everything has a lesson. But how many took the time to look and listen? How many understood that to seek after God brought

wonder and joy to a life and made all the other things pass
away?

*I have loved the shepherd's life, Lord. I have loved being
alone in the pasturelands, drinking in Your creation, watching over Your sheep. Unlike life in Bethel amid the mess and
chaos of humanity, life is simple here. People are complex
and yet simple. They want their own way! They fashion idols
they think allow them to descend into dark passions and self-
centered existence. They use the creative abilities You gave
them to make new gods that can neither punish nor rescue
them. For a while, I saw them as sheep. But they are even
more foolish and bent on destruction than these animals. Is
this love I feel for them even a spark of what You have felt
from the beginning? You are the shepherd on high, calling out
to us, "Come home! Come back to Me! Return to the fold
where you will be safe and loved!" You sing songs of deliverance every day through the wind, the birds, the night sounds.*

If only we would listen.

"We must go wherever God sends us, Hosea." If God
called him back to Israel, Amos would not argue this time.
He would go without hesitation. He would speak again
though it would mean beatings, imprisonment, even
death. How had God brought him to this point of surren-
der, stubborn, wayward man that he had been? Israel had
not turned back from rebellion, but the Lord had done a
mighty work in him.

Hosea walked, head down. "What the Lord has told me
to do is against everything in me."

"And in the midst of it, the Lord will be with you. You
will learn to pour compassion on the one who hates you."

Hosea's eyes glistened with tears. "And will I destroy
the one I love in the end as God says He will destroy us?"

Amos paused and leaned heavily on his staff. He was a simple man, not a philosopher; a shepherd, not a priest with years of study behind his opinions. "I don't know the answers, Hosea. But in the years I spent in Bethel, I knew it was not God's hatred of men that sent me there, but His great love. It is sin He hates because sin kills. Sin separates us from God, and He wants us close. In His fold." He looked out over his flock. "Sometimes it is the simple act of grazing that gets a sheep into trouble. Nibble a little here, a little there, a little more over in another area, and pretty soon, they are far from the shepherd. And then a lion comes. Or wolves. How many times over the centuries has God rescued us from our own stupidity?" He shook his head. "Too many times to count."

Will we never learn, Lord? Will our hearts never change? Would You have to make us into new creatures for us to follow You?

He went after a sheep who headed for some brush. Hosea watched. When the sheep was safely back among the others, Amos returned to him.

"A shepherd sometimes has to discipline a wayward sheep. Some are bent upon going their own way. They will go into gullies and into brambles, and lead others to death right along with them. I've had to kill a few sheep to keep the rest safe."

"As God will a few of us."

"More than a few, my friend."

"How can God love us so much and yet unleash cruel, despotic enemies upon us?"

"I've asked the same question, Hosea, and I have no answers. But I know this. The fault of much of what is coming upon us is due to our own choices. We worshiped out of habit. We gave because it was required in order to do business. In our ignorance, we equated corrupt priests with God. Or I did. We are destroyed by our own ignorance, and yet how few have the desire to learn the truth that will save them." Amos sighed. "But I talk about things I don't know or understand. If I could explain everything, would God be God? I never stood before the people of Bethel and spoke my own ideas. I spoke only the words God gave me. Anything else would have been sin. I hated the people in the beginning. In truth, I preferred the company of sheep to men. The sights, the sounds, the smells of Bethel's populace assaulted me from every side. It took a few years for God to pry open my eyes so that I could see them as lost sheep."

He shook his head. "Some things will be beyond our understanding. Even the animals know their owner and appreciate his care, but not God's people. No matter what He does for them, they still refuse to understand. Does a sheep tell the shepherd what to do? Why should man feel he can tell God what to do? But the impossibility of it all doesn't stop our people from trying. God won't let man have his way, so he carves an idol of wood or stone, props it up, and bows down to it. And his god has all the power of a scarecrow guarding a field of melons. I wanted my way for a long time, Hosea, but God had His way with me in the end." His eyes filled with tears. "And I thank God for it! I thank God every day!"

"But God is sending us with such different messages."

"Is He? Are they really that different? Surely salvation is near to those who honor Him. God's unfailing love and truth are one, and a life lived in striving for righteousness brings peace."

"Not always."

Amos knew Hosea meant to remind him of the ways in which he had suffered during his ten years in Bethel. "Is it peace with men that matters most, my friend? Or peace with God? I told the people the consequences of sin. Perhaps it is your work to show God's grace and mercy if they repent."

"I don't think I can do what He asks."

"You can't. Neither could I. I am a shepherd. I tend sheep and prune sycamore figs. Who would think me equipped or even worthy to preach God's Word in Bethel? Yet God made it so. I could say or do nothing until the Spirit of the Lord came upon me, and then anything was possible. God will make it possible for you to do the task He's given you. Your work is to trust Him."

"Will you go back to Bethel with me?"

Amos saw the hope—and fear—in Hosea's eyes. He shook his head. "No. This is where God wants me. For now." Hosea would have to rely on the Lord to complete his mission. And the Lord would be there with him at all times.

Hosea smiled ruefully. "I didn't think you would agree, Amos, but I had to ask. No man wants to be alone."

"You won't be."

Hosea understood and nodded. "I will remember you. Your courage. Your obedience. I will remember what you said and heed well the warning."

"And I will pray for you and continue to pray for all those you are sent to serve."

They embraced.

You call Your prophets to a hard life of pain and suffering, Lord.

The Spirit moved within him, and Amos knew God suffered far more than any man could imagine. The One who
created man, the One who molded and loved him into
existence was treated like a cast-off lover. *You suffer more,
Father, for Your love is greater*.

Amos's throat tightened. He bowed his head. *Oh, may
the words of my heart be pleasing to You, Lord, for You are
my Shepherd*.

When he raised his head, Amos looked north and saw
Hosea standing on the top of the hill. They raised hands to
one another, and then Hosea disappeared over the horizon.

Israel refused to heed the warnings. Would they also
scorn love?

Tears ran down Amos's cheeks, for he knew the
answer.

✦   ✦   ✦

Amos brought the flocks back to Tekoa and wintered them
in the protected pastures and shelters of home. Leaving his
trusted servants in charge, he went up to Jerusalem to
worship in the Temple and visit his brothers.

Bani told him the news. "King Zechariah has been assassinated in Samaria."

Ahiam poured feed into a manger. "He was struck
down in his capital right in front of the people. And his
assassin, Shallum, is now king of Israel."

The Word of the Lord given to Jehu all those years ago
had been fulfilled, and Jeroboam's dynasty had not lasted
past the fourth generation. In fact, Zechariah had lasted
only six months, and no other member of the family of
Jeroboam remained alive to retake power from the
crowned usurper.

Within a month, Amos heard from a merchant passing through Tekoa on his way to Jerusalem that Shallum had been executed and still another king was on the throne of Israel.

"Menahem refused to bow down to an assassin. So he came up to Samaria from Tirzah, killed Shallum, and crowned himself king of Israel."

And so a terrorist always claims a noble excuse for murder.

Having turned away from the loving-kindness of God, the people now lived under the shadow of a murderer.

And worse would come.

✦   ✦   ✦

With each day that passed, Amos's sense of foreboding grew. He had killed a lion four days ago, and heard wolves last night, but there was something else, something even more ominous in the air. He kept the sheep close, his gaze moving to any disturbance.

A man came over the hill.

Amos raised his hand to shade his eyes. It was not Elkanan or Ithai or Eliakim. The man kept walking toward Amos with purposeful strides. When Amos recognized him, he knew why he had come.

"Paarai."

"Greetings, Prophet."

Strange that fear should leave him now. Amos inclined his head, his mouth curving in a bleak smile. "How does your father fare these days?"

"My father is the one who sent me." Paarai drew a sword.

Amos had faced far worse than this arrogant young

braggart. He could easily have defended himself with his club. But he did nothing. "What do you think you will accomplish by murdering me?"

"Your prophecies die with you! Our family will remain in power. And you will be food for the buzzards!"

Amos grasped the one last opportunity given him to speak the truth. "You're wrong." Amos dropped his staff and club and spread his arms. "Kill me if you think you must, but know this. Men plan, but God prevails. The Word of the Lord will stand. And everything will happen just as God had me say it!"

Paarai cried out in rage and thrust his sword into Amos's stomach. He leaned forward, using both hands to push the blade all the way through and then let go and stepped back. Amos couldn't breathe through the pain. Looking down, he grasped the bloody hilt and sank to his knees.

"Who holds the power now?" Paarai ground out. Uttering a guttural cry of rage, he put his heel to Amos's chest and shoved him back. The blade thrust upward, slicing Amos's hands. He lay on his back, writhing in pain. "This is what you get for making a better man than you suffer! My father will be able to sleep now! He will be able to eat! He will no longer fear your words ringing in his ears!"

Standing over him, Paarai pulled the sword out slowly. Amos cried out in agony, and saw that Paarai relished it.

He knelt at Amos's side. Leaning over, he gave a feral grin, eyes black with triumph. "I'm going to leave you here now to suffer. Pray you die before a lion comes. Or the wolves. It gives me pleasure to think of your flesh being torn by hungry animals!" He stood, spit on him, and cursed him by the gods of Bethel. After kicking dust into Amos's face, he walked away. Paarai scooped up a handful of rocks, flung them at Amos's sheep, and laughed as they ran in panic.

Amos tried to rise and couldn't. When he turned his head, he saw the sheep scattering. Tears filled his eyes. He cried in pain and despair as the sun set and his lifeblood soaked into the ground. He heard the wolves and saw them gathering on the hillside. The sheep moved restlessly, no shepherd to guide or protect them.

Like Israel.

And the nations will gather around the hills of Samaria. . . .

Amos wept. *By Your mercy, I will not live to see it happen.*

Had his father once said to him that the righteous often pass away before their time because the Lord protects those He loves from the evil that is to come?

A wolf came close, crouching low, growling. Amos was helpless to protect himself. His strength was gone. The wolf came a foot closer and then bolted away, frightened by something unseen.

A gentle breeze stirred the grass. It would be night soon. Darkness was closing in. Amos felt himself lifted by strong arms. He looked into a face he had never seen before and yet his soul recognized. "Oh!" Joy filled him and he kept his eyes fixed upon the One he loved.

"Do not fear." Tears fell upon Amos's face. "All that has been said will come to pass. And then I will restore the fallen house of David. I will rebuild its ruins and restore it so that the rest of humanity might seek Me, including the Gentiles—all those I have called to be Mine."

The hope of salvation filled Amos, but he had not the strength left even to smile.

The Lord kissed his forehead. "Rest, Amos. Rest, My good and faithful servant."

Amos closed his eyes as the Good Shepherd carried him home.

NOT long after Amos died, his prophecies began to come true.

The town of Tappuah and all the surrounding country-side as far as Tirzah rebelled against Menahem. In retribution, Menahem sacked the city, killing men, women, and children, and even going so far as to follow the brutal Assyrian custom of ripping open the bellies of pregnant women and thus annihilating the next generation.

King Menahem reigned for ten years, and then the Assyrian king, Tiglath-pileser, invaded Israel and forced Menahem to pay thirty-seven tons of silver. He extorted the money from the rich of Israel. Upon Menahem's death, his son Pekahiah ascended the throne, only to be assassinated two years later by Pekah, the commander of his army. Pekah then declared himself king of Israel.

Twenty years passed as the people fell deeper into pagan worship. Hosea the prophet obeyed God's command to marry a prostitute. Time after time, Hosea took his wife back, but the people around him failed to understand the living parable of God's love for wayward Israel.

King Tiglath-pileser attacked again and captured the major cities and primary regions, taking the people captive to Assyria. Among them were Amaziah and his son, their wives left behind to fend for themselves as prostitutes.

Pekah was soon deposed by Hoshea who reigned in Samaria for nine years before King Shalmaneser of Assyria defeated him and plundered the country. When King Hoshea attempted to enlist the help of King So of Egypt, the King of Assyria returned, besieged Samaria, and razed it.

Just as Amos and other prophets warned, Israel was devoured by war. Assyrian wolves preyed upon the sheep of Israel. Those who survived were led away to foreign lands, leaving enemies to enjoy the bounty of the land God had given them. Dispersed, the ten tribes disappeared.

Judah repented under the reigns of King Hezekiah and King Josiah, but all too soon the southern kingdom also turned away from the Lord. One hundred and sixty-four years after Amos's death, Babylon invaded and conquered Judea. As the people were led away to slavery, Babylonians stripped Solomon's Temple and tore it down stone by stone.

Only then did the people repent and cry out to the Lord, and God heard their prayers.

Seventy years later, the Lord fulfilled His promise to bring them home.

For from Judah would come the Messiah. And on His shoulders would rest the government that would never end, and He would be called Wonderful Counselor, Mighty God, Everlasting Father, Prince of Peace. Jesus, the Christ, God the Son, would be the Good Shepherd who would save His people and lead them into the folds of the Lord God Almighty.

DEAR READER,

You have just finished reading the story of Amos the prophet, as told by Francine Rivers. As always, it is Francine's desire for you the reader to delve into God's Word for yourself to find out the real story—to discover what God has to say to us today and to find applications that will change our lives to suit His purposes for eternity.

Amos was a humble shepherd and gardener. His heart for God helped him to weather the times he lived in and to face rejection. Amos did not shrink from the task to which God called him. Rather, he stepped forward and embraced his calling. Amos's obedience to God's call on his life is extraordinary. It foreshadows another prophet—the ultimate Prophet, Jesus of Nazareth.

May God bless you and help you to discover his call on your life. May you discover a heart of obedience beating within you.

Peggy Lynch

SEEK GOD'S WORD FOR TRUTH
Read the following passage:

> This message was given to Amos, a shepherd from the town
> of Tekoa in Judah. He received this message in visions two
> years before the earthquake, when Uzziah was king of
> Judah and Jeroboam II, the son of Jehoash, was king of
> Israel. . . .
>
> Then Amaziah, the priest of Bethel, sent a message to Jero-
> boam, king of Israel: "Amos is hatching a plot against you
> right here on your very doorstep! What he is saying is intol-
> erable. He is saying, 'Jeroboam will soon be killed, and the
> people of Israel will be sent away into exile.'"
>
> Then Amaziah sent orders to Amos: "Get out of here, you
> prophet! Go on back to the land of Judah, and earn your
> living by prophesying there! Don't bother us with your
> prophecies here in Bethel. This is the king's sanctuary and
> the national place of worship!"
>
> But Amos replied, "I'm not a professional prophet, and
> I was never trained to be one. I'm just a shepherd, and
> I take care of sycamore-fig trees. But the LORD called me
> away from my flock and told me, 'Go and prophesy to my
> people in Israel.'"   AMOS 1:1; 7:10-15

Who was Amos and where was he from? What was his profession
and sideline?

When and how was Amos called to be a prophet? What kind of prophet was he? What kind of training did he have?

How was Amos received by the religious leaders, and why? How was he received by the political leaders?

How did Amos respond to the religious and political leaders? How did he respond to God?

FIND GOD'S WAYS FOR YOU
Who are you and what kind of training do you have?

God knew his people in advance, and he chose them to become like his Son, so that his Son would be the firstborn among many brothers and sisters. And having chosen them, he called them to come to him. And having called them, he

gave them right standing with himself. And having given
them right standing, he gave them his glory.

ROMANS 8:29-30

According to these verses, to what has God called you and why?

What is your response to God? Explain.

STOP AND PONDER

Remember, dear brothers and sisters, that few of you were
wise in the world's eyes or powerful or wealthy when God
called you. Instead, God chose things the world considers
foolish in order to shame those who think they are wise.
And he chose things that are powerless to shame those who
are powerful. . . . As a result, no one can ever boast in the
presence of God.   1 CORINTHIANS 1:26-29

SEEK GOD'S WORD FOR TRUTH
Read the following passage:

This is what the LORD says:

"The people of Damascus have sinned again and again,
    and I will not let them go unpunished!
They beat down my people in Gilead
    as grain is threshed with iron sledges.
So I will send down fire on King Hazael's palace,
    and the fortresses of King Ben-hadad will be destroyed.
I will break down the gates of Damascus. . . .
I will destroy the ruler in Beth-eden,
    and the people of Aram will go as captives to Kir,"
    says the LORD.

This is what the LORD says:

"The people of Gaza have sinned again and again,
    and I will not let them go unpunished!
They sent whole villages into exile,
    selling them as slaves to Edom.
So I will send down fire on the walls of Gaza,
    and all its fortresses will be destroyed.
I will slaughter the people of Ashdod. . . .
Then I will turn to attack Ekron,
    and the few Philistines still left will be killed,"
    says the Sovereign LORD.

This is what the LORD says:

"The people of Tyre have sinned again and again,
    and I will not let them go unpunished!
They broke their treaty of brotherhood with Israel,
    selling whole villages as slaves to Edom.

So I will send down fire on the walls of Tyre,
  and all its fortresses will be destroyed."

This is what the LORD says:

"The people of Edom have sinned again and again,
  and I will not let them go unpunished!
They chased down their relatives, the Israelites, with swords,
  showing them no mercy.
In their rage, they slashed them continually
  and were unrelenting in their anger.
So I will send down fire on Teman,
  and the fortresses of Bozrah will be destroyed."

This is what the LORD says:

"The people of Ammon have sinned again and again,
  and I will not let them go unpunished!
When they attacked Gilead to extend their borders,
  they ripped open pregnant women with their swords.
So I will send down fire on the walls of Rabbah,
  and all its fortresses will be destroyed . . . ,"
  says the LORD.

This is what the LORD says:

"The people of Moab have sinned again and again,
  and I will not let them go unpunished!
They desecrated the bones of Edom's king,
  burning them to ashes.
So I will send down fire on the land of Moab,
  and all the fortresses in Kerioth will be destroyed . . . ,"
  says the LORD.   AMOS 1:3–2:3

Name the six neighboring people/cities/nations on which Amos
pronounced God's judgment.

What did these neighbors have in common? Why was God angry
with each of them?

What judgment was decreed?

What can we learn about God from this passage?

What is implied about Amos? Explain.

FIND GOD'S WAYS FOR YOU

What similarities do you see, if any, between the behavior listed in this passage and what is going on in the world today?

> I am warning you ahead of time, dear friends. Be on guard so that you will not be carried away by the errors of these wicked people and lose your own secure footing. Rather, you must grow in the grace and knowledge of our Lord and Savior Jesus Christ.   2 PETER 3:17-18

What warnings are we given in the above passage, and why?

What are we to do to remain secure? Are you doing it?

STOP AND PONDER

> The day of the Lord will come as unexpectedly as a thief. Then the heavens will pass away with a terrible noise, and the very elements themselves will disappear in fire, and the earth and everything on it will be found to deserve judgment.   2 PETER 3:10

SEEK GOD'S WORD FOR TRUTH
Read the following passage:

This is what the LORD says:

"The people of Judah have sinned again and again,
and I will not let them go unpunished!
They have rejected the instruction of the LORD,
refusing to obey his decrees.
They have been led astray by the same lies
that deceived their ancestors.
So I will send down fire on Judah,
and all the fortresses . . . will be destroyed."

This is what the LORD says:

"The people of Israel have sinned again and again,
and I will not let them go unpunished!
They sell honorable people for silver
and poor people for a pair of sandals.
They trample helpless people in the dust
and shove the oppressed out of the way.
Both father and son sleep with the same woman,
corrupting my holy name. . . .

"So I will make you groan
like a wagon loaded down with sheaves of grain.
Your fastest runners will not get away. . . .
The archers will not stand their ground. . . .
On that day the most courageous of your fighting men
will drop their weapons and run for their lives,"
says the LORD. . . .

"My people have forgotten how to do right,"
says the LORD. . . .

"Come back to the LORD and live!
Otherwise, he will roar through Israel like a fire,
    devouring you completely. . . .
You twist justice, making it a bitter pill for the oppressed.
    You treat the righteous like dirt. . . .

"How you hate honest judges!
    How you despise people who tell the truth! . . .

"Do what is good and run from evil
    so that you may live!
Then the LORD God of Heaven's Armies will be your helper,
    just as you have claimed.
Hate evil and love what is good;
    turn your courts into true halls of justice.
Perhaps even yet the LORD God of Heaven's Armies
    will have mercy on the remnant of his people. . . .

"I hate all your show and pretense—
    the hypocrisy of your religious festivals and solemn
        assemblies. . . .

"Away with your noisy hymns of praise! . . .
Instead, I want to see a mighty flood of justice,
    an endless river of righteous living. . . ."

What sorrow awaits you who lounge in luxury . . .
    and you who feel secure . . . !
You are famous and popular . . .
    and people go to you for help. . . .
    How terrible for you. . . .

The Sovereign LORD has sworn by his own name, and this is what he, the LORD God of Heaven's Armies, says:

"I despise the arrogance of Israel,
    and I hate their fortresses.
I will give this city
    and everything in it to their enemies."
        AMOS 2:4-7, 13-16; 3:10; 5:6-7, 10, 14-15, 21, 23-24; 6:1, 4, 8

Why was God angry with Judah? with Israel?

How were the complaints against them similar to those against the surrounding people? How were they different?

What warnings were given? What judgments were promised?

What can we further learn about God from this passage?

What is implied about Amos? Explain.

FIND GOD'S WAY FOR YOU

What similarities do you see, if any, between the behavior listed in
the following passage and what is going on in our nation? our
churches? our homes?

> Get rid of all evil behavior. Be done with all deceit, hypoc-
> risy, jealousy, and all unkind speech. Like newborn babies,
> you must crave pure spiritual milk so that you will grow
> into a full experience of salvation . . . now that you have
> had a taste of the Lord's kindness.   1 PETER 2:1-3

What are we told to get rid of? What are we told to do?

What do you need to get rid of?

STOP AND PONDER

> Dear friends, I warn you as "temporary residents and for-
> eigners" to keep away from worldly desires that wage war
> against your very souls. Be careful to live properly among
> your unbelieving neighbors. Then even if they accuse you
> of doing wrong, they will see your honorable behavior, and
> they will give honor to God when he judges the world.
>   1 PETER 2:11-12

SEEK GOD'S WORD FOR TRUTH
Read the following passage:

> The Sovereign LORD showed me a vision. I saw him prepar-
> ing to send a vast swarm of locusts over the land. . . . In my
> vision the locusts ate every green plant in sight. Then I said,
> "O Sovereign LORD, please forgive us or we will not sur-
> vive, for Israel is so small."
>
> So the LORD relented from this plan. "I will not do it," he
> said.
>
> Then the Sovereign LORD showed me another vision. I saw
> him preparing to punish his people with a great fire. The
> fire had burned up the depths of the sea and was devouring
> the entire land. Then I said, "O Sovereign LORD, please stop
> or we will not survive, for Israel is so small."
>
> Then the LORD relented from this plan, too. "I will not do
> that either," said the Sovereign LORD.
>
> Then he showed me another vision. I saw the Lord stand-
> ing beside a wall that had been built using a plumb line. He
> was using a plumb line to see if it was still straight. And the
> LORD said to me, "Amos, what do you see?"
>
> I answered, "A plumb line."
>
> And the Lord replied, "I will test my people with this
> plumb line. I will no longer ignore all their sins. The pagan
> shrines of your ancestors will be ruined, and the temples of
> Israel will be destroyed; I will bring the dynasty of King
> Jeroboam to a sudden end."   AMOS 7:1-9

In what ways were the first two visions similar? How were they
different?

How did Amos respond to what the Lord had planned in these two visions? What did he ask? What was God's response?

How was the third vision different, and what was Amos's response? What significance do you see, if any, to the third vision and this response?

What can we learn about God from these visions?

What is implied about Amos? Explain.

FIND GOD'S WAYS FOR YOU

Try to recall a time when you pleaded with God on behalf of someone else.

Are any of you sick? You should call for the elders of the church to come and pray over you, anointing you with oil in the name of the Lord. Such a prayer offered in faith will heal the sick, and the Lord will make you well. And if you have committed any sins, you will be forgiven. Confess your sins to each other and pray for each other so that you may be healed. The earnest prayer of a righteous person has great power and produces wonderful results.   JAMES 5:14-16

What instructions are given in this passage? What conditions are specified?

What results are we to expect? Why?

STOP AND PONDER

The Holy Spirit helps us in our weakness. For example, we don't know what God wants us to pray for. But the Holy Spirit prays for us with groanings that cannot be expressed in words. And the Father who knows all hearts knows what the Spirit is saying, for the Spirit pleads for us believers in harmony with God's own will.   ROMANS 8:26-27

SEEK GOD'S WORD FOR TRUTH
Read the following passage:

> "I, the Sovereign LORD,
>   am watching this sinful nation of Israel.
> I will destroy it
>   from the face of the earth.
> But I will never completely destroy the family of Israel,"
>   says the LORD.
> "For I will give the command
>   and will shake Israel along with the other nations
> as grain is shaken in a sieve,
>   yet not one true kernel will be lost. . . .
>
> "In that day I will restore the fallen house of David.
>   I will repair its damaged walls.
> From the ruins I will rebuild it
>   and restore its former glory.
> And Israel will possess what is left of Edom
>   and all the nations I have called to be mine."
> The LORD has spoken,
>   and he will do these things.
>
> "The time will come," says the LORD,
> "when the grain and grapes will grow faster
>   than they can be harvested.
> Then the terraced vineyards on the hills of Israel
>   will drip with sweet wine!
> I will bring my exiled people of Israel
>   back from distant lands,
> and they will rebuild their ruined cities
>   and live in them again.
> They will plant vineyards and gardens;
>   they will eat their crops and drink their wine.
> I will firmly plant them there

> *in their own land.*
> *They will never again be uprooted*
> *   from the land I have given them,"*
> *says the LORD your God.*   AMOS 9:8-9, 11-15

Along with God's judgment to uproot and sift Israel, what did
God promise never to do?

Whose kingdom was to be restored? In what ways?

What further promise did God make to His exiled people?

What phrases are used that offered Israel hope?

What permanency did God promise Israel?

What can we learn about God from these promises?

SEEK GOD'S WAYS FOR YOU
Which of the promises of restoration listed in Amos 9 took place
for Israel? Explain.

> Humble yourselves under the mighty power of God, and at
> the right time he will lift you up in honor. . . . In his kind-
> ness God called you to share in his eternal glory by means
> of Christ Jesus. So after you have suffered a little while,
> he will restore, support, and strengthen you, and he will
> place you on a firm foundation.   1 PETER 5:6, 10

What has God promised those whom He has called? What is our
part?

In what ways has God restored, supported, or strengthened you?

STOP AND PONDER

> Oh, how great are God's riches and wisdom and knowledge!
> How impossible it is for us to understand his decisions and
> his ways!   ROMANS 11:33

AMOS AS PROPHET

> The LORD sent prophets to bring them back to him. The
> prophets warned them, but still the people would not listen.
>
> 2 CHRONICLES 24:19

According to this verse, why did God send prophets to his
people?

> Jesus told them, "A prophet is honored everywhere except
> in his own hometown and among his own family."
>
> MATTHEW 13:57

How were prophets generally treated?

> Above all, you must realize that no prophecy in Scripture
> ever came from the prophet's own understanding, or from
> human initiative. No, those prophets were moved by the
> Holy Spirit, and they spoke from God.   2 PETER 1:20-21

Who is the source of true prophecy?

AMOS AS SHEPHERD

Amos was a shepherd by profession. Read what Jesus said about shepherds in the following passage:

> The one who enters through the gate is the shepherd of the sheep. . . . The sheep recognize his voice and come to him. He calls his own sheep by name and leads them out. . . .
>
>   The good shepherd sacrifices his life for the sheep. A hired hand will run when he sees a wolf coming. He will abandon the sheep because they don't belong to him and he isn't their shepherd. . . . I am the good shepherd; I know my own sheep, and they know me.   JOHN 10:2-3, 11-12, 14

How might Amos's experience as a shepherd have prepared him to be one of God's prophets? How would his shepherding knowledge have helped him respond to God's call?

AMOS AS GARDENER

In addition to his work as a shepherd, Amos also tended fig trees. Read what Jesus said about gardeners in the following passage:

> [The gardener] cuts off every branch . . . that doesn't produce fruit, and he prunes the branches that do bear fruit so they will produce even more. . . . A branch cannot produce fruit if it is severed from the vine.   JOHN 15:2, 4

How might caring for trees have helped Amos understand the need for God's judgment?

How would it have prepared him to obey God regardless of what others thought?

AMOS AND JESUS

Amos was an obedient man. His shepherding prepared him to prod people in a caring way. His gardening skills allowed him to see that people, like plants, need to have the wild, unproductive growth removed in order to produce fruit. His obedience—along with his training—foreshadows another prophet, Jesus. Jesus said, "I am the good shepherd" (John 10:14) and "I am the true grapevine, and my Father is the gardener" (John 15:1).

In Revelation we find Jesus' prophetic warning and promise to the churches:

> Look, I am coming soon! Blessed are those who obey the words of prophecy written in this book. . . . Look, I am coming soon, bringing my reward with me to repay all people according to their deeds. . . . I, Jesus, have sent my angel to give you this message for the churches. I am both the source of David and the heir to his throne. I am the bright morning star. . . . Yes, I am coming soon!
>
> REVELATION 22:7, 12, 16, 20

May Jesus be heard in our world, our nation, our churches, our homes. May we each hear and heed His call before He comes!

FRANCINE RIVERS has been writing for almost thirty years. From 1976 to 1985 she had a successful writing career in the general market and won numerous awards. After becoming a born-again Christian in 1986, Francine wrote *Redeeming Love* as her statement of faith.

Since then, Francine has published numerous books in the CBA market and has continued to win both industry acclaim and reader loyalty. Her novel *The Last Sin Eater* won the ECPA Gold Medallion, and three of her books have won the prestigious Romance Writers of America RITA Award.

Francine says she uses her writing to draw closer to the Lord, that through her work she might worship and praise Jesus for all He has done and is doing in her life.

BOOKS BY BELOVED AUTHOR
FRANCINE RIVERS

The Mark of the Lion Series
(available individually or boxed set)
A Voice in the Wind
An Echo in the Darkness
As Sure as the Dawn

The Atonement Child
The Scarlet Thread
The Last Sin Eater
Leota's Garden
The Shoe Box

A Lineage of Grace Series
Unveiled
Unashamed
Unshaken
Unspoken
Unafraid

And the Shofar Blew

Sons of Encouragement Series
The Priest
The Warrior
The Prince
The Prophet
The Scribe (Summer 2007)